FROM A SEALED MANUSCRIPT LEFT
BEHIND AFTER DR. WATSON'S DEATH
AND ONLY NOW MADE PUBLIC AS
*THE LAST SHERLOCK HOLMES STORY*:

I was prepared for horror, but for the sight that
met my eyes there could be no preparation. At
first glance it suggested some appalling natural
disaster. Was it possible, I wondered, for a person
to explode? Then, with sickening certainty, I recognised this mess of strewn flesh as the woman I
had seen drinking and talking with Sherlock Holmes
a few hours before . . .

In that awful moment, Watson began to understand the enormity of Jack the Ripper's criminal
intent. And the mortal danger to his dear friend,
Sherlock Holmes. And to himself!

# THE LAST
# SHERLOCK HOLMES
# STORY

Michael Dibdin

BALLANTINE BOOKS • NEW YORK

Library of Congress Catalog Card Number: 77-88773

ISBN 0-345-28067-9

This edition published by arrangement with Pantheon Books

Manufactured in the United States of America

First Ballantine Books Edition: May 1979

'When William Gillette, the American actor, asked the author if he might introduce a love interest in the Sherlock Holmes play . . . Sir Arthur briskly cabled: "Marry him, murder him, do what you like with him." It should be recorded that some enthusiasts regarded even this high canonical (Conanical?) authority with disfavour.'

JAMES EDWARD HOLROYD,
introduction to
*Seventeen Steps to 221 B*

# Contents

# Foreword

On the 16th of February 1926, John Herbert Watson, M.D.—better known to millions as the 'Dr Watson' of Arthur Conan Doyle's Sherlock Holmes stories—died of injuries sustained in a fall at his home near Lyndhurst in Hampshire. He was seventy-three. When his will came to be read it was found that in a codicil he had provided for a box of papers to be left on deposit with his bankers for a period of not less than fifty years, at the end of which time it was to be opened and the contents made public.

The world in which Watson grew up had already been swept away by the Great War, in which he himself played a small but honourable role. Soon the brash unstable world that replaced it was in turn weighed in the balances and found wanting. From its smouldering ashes, after forty years of labour pains, the twentieth century was finally born. The new age grew to adolescence and then to manhood. It overran the earth, changing whatever it touched out of all recognition. This infant prodigy was celebrating its thirtieth birthday when, in the summer of 1976, a dented metal dispatch-box was duly brought up—like treasure from some fabled wreck—out of the vaults where it had lain silently for half a century. No one had any idea what it contained. The consensus of opinion was that the papers represented the unpublished notes of those cases on which Watson had collaborated with Sherlock Holmes, and which for various reasons had not previously been made public. Interest therefore ran high in the sombre panelled office where the manager of the bank, in the presence of Watson's great-nephew, raised the battered lid bearing the words 'John H. Watson, M.D., Late Army Medical Department'. The box was found to contain, together with various items of purely personal interest, a wax-sealed package of 164 typed foolscap pages, signed, and dated October 1922.

One thing was immediately evident: the document left by Dr Watson was not a collection of notes but one continuous narrative. After some discussion it was decided that the best course would be to read this aloud to the assembled company, so that its import could be judged. Thus it came about that what one of the stunned audience later termed 'a criminological time-bomb' made its public debut in the punctilious tones of an elderly man of finance. The force of the explosion was in no way diminished thereby. Within a few days of that momentous reading, rumours began to circulate about the exact nature of the revelations contained in 'the Watson papers'. At about the same time, a powerful and energetic lobby was formed by various parties united only in their determination that the papers should never be published. Their methods were both cunning and resourceful, ranging from personal persuasion to attempted arson. One of our better-known Holmesians submitted a long letter in which he successively disclosed what he called the 'well-documented fact' that Watson was 'practically a delusional psychotic from 1919 onwards', pleaded that 'a veil of discretion be drawn over his pathetic ravings', protested that publication 'would be as preposterous as the BBC interviewing some maniac who claims to be Napoleon', and finally threatened us with 'the very real possibility of prolonged and costly litigation if this lunatic libel ever sees the light of day'. Fortunately not all the correspondence we received was this strident. We particularly cherish a letter from one S. Holmes of Sussex, who vehemently denied reports of his death while extolling the virtues of a 'miracle diet' based on royal jelly, his monograph on which he was prepared to let us publish at a mutually acceptable fee!

There can be no question that the contents of this book will prove extremely controversial. Many people will be deeply shocked by the nature of Watson's statement. Many will no doubt prefer to reject it rather than surrender the beliefs of a lifetime. Others will at least regret that two of the great mysteries of crime are finally solved, and will seek to discredit the solution. It is true that Watson's claims can no longer be substantiated. But every one of his references to a known event has been checked by our research team against the facts—many of which were not publicly available in 1922—and we can certify that no obvious anomalies exist. The detractors may say what they like, but they cannot deny that the present version fits the evidence. That it is true is at the very least possible. We believe that on mature consideration many readers may come to share our conviction that it is in fact extremely probable.

The preparation of the typescript for the press has not been onerous. Editorial intervention has been restricted to the silent correction of a few solecisms, the division of the original into chapters, and the provision of some indispensable footnotes. Apart from these gentle ministrations the work has been left to speak for itself—as, despite the author's protests, it so very effectively does.

THE EDITORS

# Introduction

*It was the autumn of 1888, and the day one of that class that Sherlock Holmes used to describe as 'unhealthy'. The sky was a dreary grey presaging the rain that fell limply in intermittent showers. There was hardly a breath of wind. At that time I was still sharing rooms in Baker Street with Holmes, and on the morning of which I speak we had just concluded breakfast. Now I stood smoking a cigarette and staring down from the bow-window at the street below. Holmes lay sprawled in his armchair before the empty grate, a newspaper open on his knees and a pipe clenched between his teeth. Though gloomy, the weather was too close for us to light a fire and bring some cheer to our dismal chambers. At length the silence was broken by Holmes's exclamation of disgust. He tossed the paper aside, and his long bloodless fingers snaked up towards the cocaine-bottle and the needles. At that very moment the bell rang. There was a muttered exchange below and then a rush of footsteps on the stairs. Our door flew open and—*

No, this really won't do. I thought it might give my story a little more conviction if I tried at least to echo A.C.D., but I cannot even manage that. Ah, what a thing he would make of it! Gripping the reader with his

1

opening words and sweeping him off on a brisk guided tour of the plot; getting the dates wrong, falling over the facts, confusing the names, and all with such sheer panache that no one would dream of asking awkward questions, or of doubting for a moment that what they were hearing was the whole truth and nothing but. Whereas I will probably be dismissed as a senile dreamer and a bungling purveyor of ill-told tales. But then it is none of my business to try and convince anyone. I leave that to the men of letters. I am a doctor and a soldier; all I can do is make my report.

But at once I run up against a problem which A.C.D. never dreamed of—I cannot know who is reading this. These words will not see print before 1972, at the earliest. What manner of men will walk the earth at that fabulous date? Will any of this matter to you? Perhaps no one then will even have heard of Jack the Ripper, or of Sherlock Holmes either. How can I know? Nevertheless, I must go on, and if I say too much or too little for your understanding, you will no doubt pardon an old man living out his days in a barbarous age—an age of darkness. For my part, I will try not to take too much for granted. No one now seems to read Clark Russell;* in fifty years A.C.D.'s work may likewise have passed into oblivion. But no doubt some energetic editor can exhume the Holmes stories from one of our larger libraries, and append to this text such sections as may be necessary to complete the sense. What even the energetic editor will not be able to discover, and what I must therefore explain before going any further, is the connection between the stories and the reality, and the circumstances under which they came to be written.

I had been living with Sherlock Holmes for almost four years when I was first introduced to A.C.D. through a mutual acquaintance in the medical world.

---

*William Clark Russell (1844–1911) was a prolific and popular writer of adventure stories with a maritime setting. He was apparently one of Dr Watson's favourite authors. Swinburne referred to him as 'the greatest master of the sea, living or dead', but his reputation has not survived.

He was then just setting up in practice at Southsea, near Portsmouth, and we met during one of his all-too-infrequent trips to town. We got on at once. For one thing we shared a common medical interest, but there was more to it than that. Perhaps Holmes summed it up best, with the mordant wit so characteristic of him, when he remarked that A.C.D. was something more than just a general practitioner, while I was something less. A bond was formed between us at all events, and during Holmes's absence some time later I invited A.C.D. to dine at Baker Street. It proved to be a splendid evening, and the first of many others. A.C.D. regaled me with a succession of interesting anecdotes (I particularly recall a humorous account of his misadventures in a joint practice at Plymouth) and I in my turn related some pretty hair-raising experiences from my time in Afghanistan. Surrounded as we were on every side by the evidence of my fellow-lodger's eccentric pursuits, it was inevitable that the talk should at last come round to him. Sherlock Holmes was at that time virtually unknown outside the closed circles frequented by the police force and the criminal class. The public at large had hardly heard of him, for he took care that his name did not appear in the reports of the cases he undertook. I was thus in the happy position of having virgin territory up my conversational sleeve, so to speak. I recounted my adventures in Holmes's company, I recalled examples of his almost uncanny powers of deduction and inference, I posed impenetrable mysteries and then effortlessly demonstrated how Holmes had solved them. A.C.D. was visibly impressed by all this, but I naturally had no inkling that the man who kept me up into the small hours with his questions and comments was to be the author of Holmes's present international fame.

Though that evening's entertainment had sparked an idea in A.C.D.'s mind, nothing was to come of it for another two years. Holmes remained a topic of conversation whenever we got together, but it was not until the summer of 1887—a date that now seems as remote and

unreal as 1972—that I realised that A.C.D.'s interest
was anything more than conversational. I had been invited to spend a few days at Southsea, and had readily
accepted, for London was like an oven. One afternoon,
as the three of us (A.C.D. was by then married) were
taking tea in the garden, A.C.D. made me a proposal. It
seemed that he had already tried his hand at writing,
and had met with moderate success. He now thought it
might be possible to do something based on one of
Holmes's cases. What he had in mind was an entirely
new type of story that would combine both fact and fiction. The basis of the piece would be fact, drawn from
the notes I kept of Holmes's most interesting cases, but
the manner would be that of fiction, employing all the resources of dialogue and narrative art. A.C.D. wished
me to approach Holmes and sound out his willingness
to sanction this scheme. This I very gladly agreed to do.
I had long regretted Holmes's lack of the fame and fortune I felt to be his due. Here, surely, was a capital
means to supply it. I raised the matter immediately
upon my return to Baker Street. Holmes listened in silence while I explained A.C.D.'s proposition. When I
had done, he took up his cherry-wood pipe and smoked
quietly for several minutes more. Finally he spoke.

'Is he able, this friend of yours?'

'His name is not yet upon everybody's lips,' I replied,
'but his work has found ready acceptance in a wide
range of periodicals. When the *Cornhill* printed a story
of his incognito, one critic took it to be the work of
Stevenson!'

Holmes snorted. 'Pooh! It is not of the slightest interest to me whether the man can sell ten thousand
magazines with some fictional frippery. What I need to
know is whether he can set down ten plain facts without
tricking them out in some guise more attractive than
that in which they actually appeared.'

'I have every confidence in his ability to do justice to
whichever case you see fit to offer him,' I returned a
trifle stiffly.

Holmes seemed not to have heard. 'Will he be content to let the story tell itself?' he mused. 'Does he have the humility to follow in my footsteps, telling each link of the iron chain of cause and effect by which I force the truth to reveal itself? In a word, can he leave well enough alone?'

I was silent. Holmes glanced at me, and then looked back into the blazing fire, as though the answers to his questions were to be sought there.

'Do you have some particular case in mind?' said he at last.

'Well I naturally wished to consult you before coming to any decision. But I confess my first thought was of the Roylott affair, or possibly the Hope case.'

'The former is out of the question, I fear. I gave Miss Stoner quite explicit assurances that her privacy would be respected.'*

'Then the other, if you agree. No one's interests can be at stake there.'

'Except my own, of course. Well, you have my *imprimatur*. Send all the details we possess concerning Mr Jefferson Hope down to Southsea, and let us see what comes of it.'

I did so the very next day, with results that are known to the world. What is not known is Holmes's response to A.C.D.'s 'A Study in Scarlet'. I must admit that I felt at once that the title was not going to meet with my friend's approval. His own suggestion, duly passed on by me, had been 'Towards a Definitive Praxis of Applied Criminal Anthropology: Some Notes on the Stangerson–Drebber Murders of 1881'. Apart from this detail, however, I felt that even Holmes could find nothing of which to complain. A.C.D. had presented the case in the form of an extract from my (non-existent, of course) *Reminiscences*—thereby creating for me a literary reputation upon which I was to dine out modestly in later years. But within this fictional

---

*The affair of Miss Helen Stoner and her stepfather Dr Grimesby Roylott was, however, to be made public four years later in the adventure of 'The Speckled Band'.

shell the yolk of fact had been preserved unbroken. Of course, A.C.D. had not been pedantic about it. He had altered various circumstantial details in the interests of dramatic tension, and had also added a long section of his own invention to provide a suitably grim motive for Hope's revenge. But I felt that all his improvements were well within the bounds of artistic licence, and I looked forward to Holmes's approbation of our joint venture.

I myself was completely entranced by the piece. I purchased my copy in Oxford Street, and started reading it on the way home. Having twice narrowly escaped being knocked down by indignant pedestrians, I took refuge in a nearby public garden and finished the piece just as the light was failing. I had been reading for over three hours without the slightest awareness of the passage of time. I hurried home to Baker Street, eager to share my satisfaction with Holmes. To my great surprise, I found him already clutching a copy of the very publication in which I had been immersed all afternoon.

He looked up sharply as I entered. 'Well, Watson, and where have you been? Sitting outside, eh? In Manchester Square garden, unless I'm very much mistaken. Hardly the season for that, I would have thought. Could it be that you were ashamed to come home, having seen how your precious doctor of letters has bungled his work?'

'Ashamed, Holmes? Certainly not! I must say I hardly expected this! As for the story, I think it's rather swell.'

It was an unfortunate choice of words, but the American idiom employed by A.C.D. in the latter half of his tale had told on my vocabulary. Holmes glanced at me keenly, and I felt the iron enter my soul.

' "Swell"? Hm! Not, I must confess, the first term that occurred to me. But perhaps not inappropriate, if you intend to suggest something swollen and bloated, something puffed up out of all recognition, a hideous perversion of everything I stand for—'

'But Holmes—'

'I was quite prepared for some degree of misrepresentation. I had resigned myself to expect a certain lack of fidelity in his reproduction of the finer details. I was not sanguine upon the probability of seeing my methods and principles exemplified in all their full complexity.'

'But Holmes—'

'On the other hand, I was by no means ready to see my investigation made the occasion for the most grotesque and least necessary excrescence to have erupted on the literary scene since the invention of the printing-press.'

'But Holmes—'

'I wonder if your colleague's medical prowess partakes of the same genius which guides his pen? If so, I pity his patients. I shall not be in the least surprised to hear that he has amputated a man's leg because he complained of heartburn. A mere prescription of bicarbonate of soda would naturally be too prosaic to satisfy Mr Doyle's taste for the sensational.'

'But Holmes, what has he done to deserve this? He has demonstrated admirably your unparalleled powers of investigation. He has shown you succeeding where the authorities failed. He has celebrated the complete triumph of your methods and techniques. What more can you possibly ask?'

'Nothing more, Watson, but quite a bit less. For a start, what is this schoolboy yarn about deserts of salt and murderous Mormons doing stuck in the middle of my case, like a putty nose on an antique bust?'

'Come, he had to dramatise—'

'Did he, indeed? How long has he suffered from this compulsion, pray? Did it come on suddenly, or did he acquire the habit by degrees? No doubt this same morbid craving explains that truly remarkable scene in which Hope, half-dead of an aneurism by the by, has to be restrained by four men from precipitating himself from our windows?'

'I see no harm in that,' I cried hotly. 'Really, Holmes! If you are going to object to every trifle! He removed the scene of the arrest from the cab-yard to our rooms simply to condense the action, thereby rendering it more effective. The thing is perfectly in order. Why, in classical drama it was a requirement! I believe the device is referred to as Unity of Place.'

Holmes smiled sweetly. 'How interesting,' he purred. 'You never cease to edify, my dear fellow. Perhaps you would be so good as to elucidate for my benefit the device—classical or otherwise, I'm not particular—which induced Jefferson Hope to present himself that evening at an address to which, not twenty-four hours earlier, he had refused to come, rightly suspecting a trap?'

This left me at a loss. To tell the truth, I had fallen under A.C.D.'s spell to such an extent that this fundamental error had wholly escaped me. Holmes observed my confusion wryly. 'Whoever belittles my opponents, belittles me,' he concluded, tossing the volume aside. 'Let us hear no more of this meddler. The association is at an end.'

I was familiar enough with Holmes's moods to recognise the futility of further argument. The subject was dropped, and I began to consider how I should break the news to A.C.D. In the event I was let off lightly. Holmes's disillusionment with 'A Study in Scarlet' was fully shared, although for very different reasons, by its author. Having had the greatest difficulty in placing it with a publication, he then had to endure an almost complete lack of interest in the product of his labours—a fate, as he told me, worse than any amount of adverse notice. Having tried out his novelty and seen it fail, he decided to turn his hand once more to a conventional product, where he soon met with considerably greater success. Thus at that time there seemed every reason to believe that the association was indeed at an end.

A.C.D. did not in fact attempt another such piece for two years. The case he then treated was that into which Holmes and I were plunged in the summer of 1888 and it is here that my own narrative has its beginning. Although the affair which A.C.D. was to call 'The Sign of Four' seemed at the time no more than another entry in the long list of mysteries which Holmes had been called upon to solve, in hindsight it is clear that it marked a watershed in Holmes's life, and in his relations with me. The reason is not far to seek, and has nothing to do with Jonathan Small, or with the Agra Treasure over which so much blood was spilt. But in the course of Holmes's investigations I met and fell in love with Mary Morstan, whose father's disappearance had set the whole train of events in motion. I was fortunate enough to find my feelings reciprocated, and in due course I was able to announce our engagement to Holmes.

His response stunned me. I had not expected him to be overjoyed at the news, but I was astonished by his inability even to dissemble his displeasure. To this day I can hear his groan, and the cold words that followed.

'I really cannot congratulate you.'

This remark was, to say the least, extremely embarrassing. I hardly knew how to reply. In the end, though, I managed to come up with some banter to the effect that everyone concerned seemed to have done well out of Holmes's success in the Sholto case, except Holmes himself.

'You have done all the work in this business,' I cried. 'As it is, I get a wife out of it, and the police get all the credit. Pray what remains for you?'

His face was set and his voice bleak as he replied.

'For me there remains the cocaine-bottle.'

How could I have overlooked the implied appeal? How could I fail to understand? I am staggered by the extent of my blindness. But then perhaps nothing I could have done would have made any difference. Perhaps what was to happen would have happened in any case. Perhaps its sources were in deeper and darker regions than those over which I ever had any influence. Perhaps. Perhaps.

This is what I tell myself. My heart tells me that I betrayed my closest friend in the hour of his need, and I know no way to answer.

# One

My notes—which I shall endeavour to follow with the minimum of extraneous comment for the remainder of this narrative—reveal that on the morning of Friday the 28th of September 1888, Sherlock Holmes received a telegram. This was in itself scarcely a remarkable occurrence. At that period telegrams were coming and going with such frequency at 221B Baker Street that I sometimes wonder how many clerks Holmes maintained in permanent employment with the welter of messages he received and dispatched. This state of affairs resulted from a problem which had been developing for several years with regard to Holmes's consulting practice.

The problem was simple, inevitable, and apparently quite insurmountable. It sprang from the fact that crime, like any other human activity, follows a limited number of patterns. Ninety-nine out of a hundred crimes are immediately recognisable to an expert as being of this type or of that. There is no mystery to be solved, no puzzle to tax the brain. All that is required to apprehend the guilty party is hard work and a little luck. Such crimes gladden the heart of the police force, whose capacity for hard work has never been in doubt, but to Holmes they were anathema. His first question on being asked to undertake an investigation was always the same: did it contain any features of interest? If so, he would happily fling all his energies into the task, be his client duchess of dustman, his fees a king's ransom or a beggar's alms. But if the requisite features of interest were absent, nothing would induce him to intervene—and if his hand were forced, as in the matter of the Aldershot scandal of '86, those responsible soon discovered to their chagrin that unless his interest was engaged, Holmes was a mere shadow of the man whose mental powers could seem almost supernatural when they were fully deployed.

Sherlock Holmes originally set up as a consulting detective in 1877, some four years before I met him. Cases were at first hard to come by, but at that time each presented a fresh challenge and was tackled with enthusiasm. Ten years later the position was very different. Like all superior intellects, Holmes disdained to cover the same ground twice, and thus a point was bound to come when he spent less time solving crimes than he did lying about our front room bemoaning the dullness and lack of enterprise of the British criminal class. At such moments he frequently put me in mind of a jaded emperor from the last days of Rome, berating his underlings for their inability to create a spectacle lavish or rare enough to divert him. It was at about this time that he began to resort to cocaine. At first the drug was nothing more than an occasional expedient to which Holmes had recourse when every other weapon for staving of *ennui* had failed him. I regarded it as a filthy habit, but still preferable to the alternative—unpredictable and savage outbursts of nervous energy in which he would assault the furniture with a horsewhip, or in some still less desirable way relieve the pent-up frustration of his soul. I vividly recall the occasion when he sat himself down with a revolver and a box of cartridges and began firing at the opposite wall, until he had improved its appearance with a script V.R. and crown executed in bullet-pocks. Holmes was a man very finely balanced between reason and hysteria. He liked to compare himself to a racing-engine, which will tear itself to pieces unless coupled to the work that it was designed to do. In the absence of such work the cocaine seemed to act as a regulator, and as such I was prepared to turn a blind eye to his use of it. It seemed at first an acceptable remedy for Holmes's chronic ailment.

But as interesting cases became less and less frequent, the occasional vice became more and more so, until at the period of which I speak Holmes was regularly injecting into his blood a solution of almost standard strength three times a day.* I do not know whether the reader is familiar with the effects of cocaine. By 1972 the drug may have passed for ever from the face or the earth, or, I suppose, be given to squalling children to quiet them. Although without the physically deleterious effect of opium, cocaine is a powerful and dangerous agent when used indiscriminately for personal pleasure, and not—as Nature surely intended—for the relief of pain. The mood of the user is at once exalted to unprecedented heights, only to be subsequently plunged into the most profound lassitude, which of itself demands a renewal of the dosage. Soon the desire for the drug becomes a vicious craving. All one's social and moral standards are undermined, for nothing can offer satisfactions to rival those freely available within the closed circle of one's own mind. In the end, the addict ceases to regard himself as a member of the human race, and by the same token he usually ceases to behave like one. The world and its denizens come to seem a pale and fraudulent imitation of his own fantasies, and he treats them much as a spoiled child treats toys which have ceased to amuse him. Such was the perilous ally to which Sherlock Holmes had turned for relief, and once I realised the extent to which he had come to depend on the drug I strove with all my might to wean him from it. But to no avail. Whatever arguments I advanced, his reply was always the same:

*The standard strength of a cocaine solution for hypodermic injection was set at 10 per cent in the British Pharmacopoeia of 1898. According to 'The Sign of Four', Holmes used a 7 per cent solution.

'My dear Watson, nothing would give me greater pleasure than to give it up. Only bring me work! Find me some problem to exercise my intellect, and you may play at darts with my needles for all I care.'

To this I had no answer. Holmes had been stalemated by his own prodigious genius. He had solved every problem, and thereby created one which appeared truly insoluble.

But though the fires burned low, they had not gone out, and since Holmes's fame was now at its zenith his advice was sought on all sides. Hence the telegrams. Every morning after breakfast he so far compromised his indolence as to read through the newspapers, cast an eye over his post, and then fire off cryptic memoranda to various destinations. 'How many rungs had the ladder?' a message might run, or 'If the milk was off, Furneaux is your man.' These oracular pronouncements were dispatched daily all over our islands, and in some cases also to the Continent. They were received generally with gratitude, occasionally with incredulity, but very rarely in vain. Holmes's inferences were almost always proved correct, and where they failed it always subsequently transpired that some fact had been distorted or withheld. Not that his vicarious triumphs appeared to afford Holmes the slightest pleasure. It was a ritual he performed each day, as one might any tedious but necessary duty, and then resumed his brown study.

I was therefore both astonished and delighted when my friend—having read the telegram of which I speak—handed a scribbled reply to the boy, gave out a brief laugh, and began to pace the floor as of old.

'Is it a case, Holmes?' I enquired hopefully. His last investigation, the Cushing horror, had been concluded more than a month before.*

'In a way,' said he, handing me the form in passing.

The telegram was from one of Holmes's old contacts at Scotland Yard. I read: 'Have you been following

*For further details of the Cushing case, see Conan Doyle's 'The Adventure of the Cardboard Box'.

these Whitechapel killings? I might call later if you are free. We have something fresh. G. Lestrade.'

I looked up in some surprise at Holmes, who chuckled.

'You may not be aware, Watson, that among my other accomplishments I have become something of an expert at interpreting the Scotland Yard dialect. It is an interesting idiom, although its relation to English as we know it is somewhat tenuous. This telegram is a good example. A tiro would never suspect that behind this mask of insouciance there hides a desperate man, a man hounded and harried by the press, by the public, and by his superiors—a man at his wits' end, begging for help! Translated into our common tongue, Lestrade's message reads: "Three women brutally murdered this past month in Whitechapel—more killings expected—all suspects released for lack of evidence—utterly baffled—you are our last hope—for God's sake say you'll see me!" '

'And did you?'

'Oh certainly. One should never miss the spectacle of the police *in loco clientis*. Besides, this case is of some considerable interest. You have heard of it, of course?'

The question was indeed purely rhetorical. There can have been no one in the kingdom that fateful autumn who was unaware of the terrible events unfolding in the East End. People could talk of nothing else.

'I really didn't imagine you would consider it worth looking into, Holmes,' I answered. 'It all seems rather sordid and disgusting. Hardly your style, I would have thought.'

'Sordid enough and disgusting enough, in all conscience, but redeemed by some quite extraordinary features of interest—as I may be able to show you. Would you have the goodness to hand me down the red volume on the topmost shelf? I must confess that Lestrade's *cri de coeur* has not come as a complete surprise to me. I have been expecting something of the sort for several weeks now, and to that end I have been compiling a few cuttings on the subject. It is never a good idea to let the constabulary feel that they have you at a disadvantage. It inflames their inherent sense of superiority. Now then, if you are agreeable, I will run over the facts as briefly and clearly as I can. This will be of the greatest benefit to me, in refreshing my grasp of the case.'

'I could wish for nothing better,' said I, and meant it most sincerely. The coolness that had sprung up between us since I announced my engagement had suddenly been dispelled. The cloud I feared had settled for ever on Holmes's spirit had suddenly lifted. The game was afoot once more!

Holmes leafed through the commonplace book with one hand, while with the other he lifted down the Persian slipper containing his tobacco.

'Let me see! "Another Ghastly Murder in Whitechapel." Hm! "Horrible Atrocities of a Maniac." Quite so! "Reign of Terror in East London." "Police Impotent." Dear me! "Fearful Scenes," "Sketches at the Inquest," "Bloodstains on the Stones." Well! The fourth estate has certainly been having a field-day. But once you skim off the froth and the *frissons,* the actual matter might be copied on to a single sheet of note-paper— such as this one. Now before examining the murders individually we should note the important features they have in common. Each of the victims was a female pauper of doubtful morals. All three were middle-aged, physically unprepossessing, and lacking even a few pence for a bed. They thus had to spend the night in the streets, where they were murdered within a few hundred yards of each other during the early hours of the morning. All of which raises the interesting question of motive, or rather the lack of it. Why should anyone wish to kill these pathetic drabs? Gain is out of the question, and the notion of any of the three being the object of a *crime passionel* is plainly grotesque. But there is another and even greater mystery, which also stamps the three killings as being the work of the same hand. In each case the weapon used was a knife, and it was wielded not merely to kill but to mutilate. The first victim, Tabram, was stabbed repeatedly in the stomach.

The other two had their throats cut and were then disembowelled. It was this that first drew my attention to the case. It makes for something distinctly out of the ordinary. Here is a cutting from the *Star,* describing the corpse of the second victim, Nicholls.'

I took the open volume from him, and read the following.

> The throat is cut in two gashes, the instrument having been a sharp one, but used in a ferocious and reckless way. There is a gash under the left ear, reaching nearly to the centre of the throat. Along half of its length, however, it is accompanied by another one which reaches around under the other ear, making a wide and horrible hole, and nearly severing the head from the body. The ghastliness of this cut, however, pales into insignificance alongside the other. No murder was ever more ferociously or more brutally done. The knife, which must have been a large and sharp one, was jabbed into the deceased at the lower part of the abdomen, and then drawn upwards, not once but twice. The first cut veered to the right, slitting up the groin, and passing over the left hip, but the second cut went straight upward, along the centre of the body, and reaching to the breast-bone.

'Good God, Holmes! What manner of man could—"

'All in good time, Watson, all in good time. I am not without my ideas, but these are deep waters. We would do well not to theorise in advance of the facts.'

'If I had not read it in the newspaper, I would not have believed it possible. In these days! In our England! Of all the infamies you have ever had to deal with, this must surely be the most abominable!'

'I do not doubt it. Certainly this killer, whoever he may be, is no common criminal. But to continue. Tabram was slain on the seventh of last month, and Nicholls on the thirty-first. Eight days later a third body was discovered, in a yard behind a house in Hanbury Street. Where are my notes of the inquest? Yes: "The throat had been severed. There were two distinct clean cuts. It appeared as though an attempt had been made to separate the bones of the neck." I quote from the evidence of Dr Philips, the police surgeon who examined the victim. "There were various other mutilations of the body but I am of the opinion that they occurred subsequent to death. I think I had better not go into further detail of these mutilations which can only be painful to the feelings of the jury and the public." Humph! Strange scruples, one might think, under the circumstances. The coroner evidently did, for when the inquest resumed he pressed the point. In the words of the *Illustrated Police News,* "witness then detailed the terrible wounds which had been inflicted upon the woman and described the parts of the body which the perpetrator of the murder had carried away with him." Which is as far as that upstanding organ, the *censor morum* of our semi-literate class, is prepared to go. Its reticence was shared by the rest of the daily press, including *The Times,* which termed Dr Philips's evidence "totally unfit for publication". Indeed, one might have been forced to appeal to Lestrade for enlightenment, were it not that you, my dear Watson, still maintain that slender link with the world of medicine: a subscription to the *Lancet.* That excellent journal was of course under no necessity of sparing its readership, and was thus able to print the unprintable section of Dr Philips's evidence.'

Once again he passed me the book, indicating with a bony finger one of the pasted cuttings.

The abdomen had been entirely laid open; the intestines, severed from their mesenteric attachments, had been lifted out of the body, and placed on the shoulder of the corpse; whilst from the pelvis the uterus and its appendages with the upper portion of the vagina and the posterior two-thirds of the bladder, had been entirely removed. No trace of these parts could be found.

'Such was the fate of the killer's third victim, Chapman,' Holmes commented. 'Do you know this Philips, by the way?'

'But why, Holmes? In God's name why?'

'My dear fellow! The medical world is a comparatively small one, after all. I thought perhaps—'

'No, no! The murders! This dreadful senseless mutilation! Why should anyone wish to do such a thing? What could it possibly profit them?'

Holmes looked up at me from the pages of his book.

'You put the matter in a nutshell, Watson. In themselves, after all, the murders are quite insignificant. Such females are killed in one way or another every week in that district, and only the registrar takes any notice. Nothing could be less inspiring to the analytical observer. But when the killer tarries by the lifeless body of his victim, deliberately risking capture in order to inflict the most fiendish mutilations on the insensible flesh, then the affair transcends its sordid content and aspires to the realm of the unique and the inspirational!'

I could hardly be expected to share Holmes's sentiments concerning these monstrous atrocities, but I knew my friend well enough not to be shocked by his callous tone. No amount of weeping or gnashing of teeth was going to bring the maniac responsible to justice. If he could be stopped, Holmes was the man to do it. But could even he bring light into such utter darkness?

'No one knows your powers better than I, Holmes, but I confess I cannot see how you hope to bring them to bear in this case. Here is no closed circle of suspects to be considered one by one, no hidden motive to betray the guilty party. This monster strikes at random, materialising out of the night to do his horrible work, and then vanishing as if by magic! Why, almost any man in London might have done the murders! Your suspects must be counted in millions!'

'Come, it's hardly as bad as that. Of those millions, many will turn out to have an alibi for at least one of the nights in question. And most of the others can be ruled out as simply constitutionally incapable of any crimes as extraordinary as these. Besides, you err in stating that the killer leaves no clues. The case is rather the reverse. Why—where is it? Yes!—Thursday's *Times* opined that "there is a perfect abundance of clues, provided they be followed up." Not only that, but

> the police will be expected to follow up with the keenest vigilance the valuable clue elicited through the coroner's inquest, and, since the lines of their investigation are plainly chalked out by information which they themselves failed to collect, it will be a signal disgrace if they do not succeed.

No wonder poor Lestrade has decided to honour us with a visit!'

'But what is this valuable clue to which they allude?'

'Well, I cannot altogether agree as to its value,' Holmes laughed. 'It seems that the coroner, in his summing-up, noted the absence of various organs from the corpse, and suggested that the motive for the killings might after all be simple financial gain. In other words—'

I gasped.

'Burke and Hare!'*

'Precisely. Resurrectionism resurrected. It is an ingenious theory, and Baxter did well to mention it. But I doubt if the police will meet with much success if they take it literally—and how else, after all, do they ever take anything? But unless I am much mistaken, here comes Lestrade to put their case in person. Are you aware that it is possible to distinguish thirty-three different trades and professions by the sound of their footsteps? I was thinking at one time of publishing a small monograph on the subject. Ah come in, Inspector! The cane chair is vacant. I gather you have finally come to

---

*William Burke and William Hare murdered at least fifteen persons in Edinburgh during 1828, selling the corpses to a local surgeon for prices ranging from £8 to £14.

seek my assistance in putting an end to these Whitechapel murders.'

Lestrade looked pained.

'I don't know where you got that idea, Mr Holmes. The fact is I just happened to be passing this way, and knowing how you interest yourself in these matters I thought to myself—'

'Quite so. Most kind, I'm sure. But do tell us how your investigation is proceeding. No doubt by now an arrest is imminent—if not indeed two or three.'

'Oh, I can't divulge that information. You can hardly expect that, Mr Holmes! This is only a private call, you know.'

'Come, come!' cried Holmes cordially. 'No need to be bashful. Don't spare my feelings! It is a blow, I admit, to learn that you are doing so well without me, but I shall get over it. Who is the guilty party? We are all agog to know.'

Lestrade scratched his mutton-chops with a well-bitten fingernail.

'I don't say we can make a case against any one person as yet. But we have our suspicions, and as soon as they are confirmed we shall not hesitate to move.'

'Of course! Very wise! After that fiasco with the Pizer fellow you will naturally want to tread warily. I understand that he is instituting legal action. It was a Sergeant Thicke who made the arrest, was it not? Strange how some names lodge in the memory.'

'What is this Holmes?' I demanded. 'Who is Pizer?'

Holmes turned to Lestrade, and indicated with a theatrical gesture that the floor was his. The official coughed and shuffled uneasily.

'John Pizer, also known as "Leather Apron", was our first suspect in the Chapman killing. A leather apron was found beside the body. This alerted our suspicions. We then learned that the woman Nicholls has been friendly with a man known by the same alias. Acting upon this information, a sergeant of H division proceeded to premises in Mulberry Street, where he effected the arrest of—'

'Unfortunately,' Holmes cut in, 'the fellow in question turned out to have an unbreakable alibi for the nights in question, and was duly released the next day.'

'It's easy to be wise after the event,' replied Lestrade with a touch of bitterness.

'True. But I should have thought it was at least obvious that the man we are looking for is not some cringing shoemaker who, hearing that he is suspected, locks himself up in his room in terror of the pogrom. However, let that be. I have no wish to dwell on your failures, my dear Inspector. Life is too short. What is the present state of your enquiries? Have you been following up Coroner Baxter's interesting suggestions?'

Lestrade sneered.

'Between you and me, Mr Holmes, the coroner would do better to stick to his job, and leave the investigation to those who are properly qualified for it.'

'I could not agree more. But no doubt he was aware that I had not been invited to participate.'

For a moment the two detectives, official and unofficial, stared at one another. Then Lestrade blinked and made a smile.

'Oh you are a wag, sir. Highly humorous. Good 'un. Ha.'

'You are too kind. But I see I am in danger of monopolising the conversation. Your wire, I believe, mentioned fresh news.'

A sly look appeared on Lestrade's face.

'What would you say if I was to tell you that I have in my pocket a letter which we believe to be from the murderer?'

If the Scotland Yarder had hoped to produce an effect, he was rewarded with a stunned silence. Holmes leant forward, now totally serious and alert.

'I would say that I would very much like to see that letter.'

Lestrade reached into his coat, producing with a flourish an envelope which he passed to Holmes. My friend drew from it a sheet of paper. He read it through with the utmost concentration, and then passed it on to me. It was a letter written in a good hand, with red ink. It ran this way:

Dear Boss,                                        25 Sept. 1888
            I keep on hearing the police have caught me, but they won't fix me just yet. I have laughed when they look so clever and talk about being on the right track. That joke about Leather Apron gave me real fits. I am down on whores and I shant quit ripping them till I do get buckled. Grand work the last job was. I gave the lady no time to squeal. How can they catch me now. I love my work and want to start again. You will soon hear of me with my funny little games. I saved some of the proper *red* stuff in a ginger beer bottle over the last job to write with but it went thick like glue and I cant use it. Red ink is fit enough I hope *ha, ha*. The next job I do I shall clip the ladys ears off and send to the police officers just for jolly wouldnt you. Keep this letter back till I do a bit more work, then give it out straight. My knife's so nice and sharp I want to get to work right away if I get a chance. Good luck.
                              Yours truly
                                        Jack the Ripper

Dont mind me giving the trade name

A few lines had been added to the letter crosswise, as a postscript.

Wasnt good enough to post this before I got all the red ink off my hands curse it. No luck yet. They say I'm a doctor now *ha ha*

I returned this extraordinary document to Holmes, who was studying the envelope intently through his magnifying glass.

'Nothing to be learned from the paper,' he murmured. 'The letter is dated the 25th, yet the postmark gives the 27th. Why did he not post it sooner? Hm!

"Keep this letter back till I do a bit more work, then give it out straight." By Jove! He was worried lest the press lack the necessary patience! You realise what this means, of course?'

Lestrade and I gazed mutely at Holmes, who rapped the letter with his fingertips.

'Why, he is as good as telling you that he will attempt another murder within the next few nights!'

'Oh, is that all?' Lestrade laughed. 'For a moment I thought you had spotted something. I can read as well as you, Mr Holmes, but why should we believe what he says? It is most likely all a trick.'

Holmes shook his head impatiently.

'Never mind what he says. Observe what he does! If he merely wished to confuse us, he would have posted the letter as soon as it was written, on Tuesday. Why should he delay? But instead he deliberately keeps the letter back until Thursday, and then urges the press not to make it public until he "gets to work again". That must mean that he knows beyond all doubt that another killing *will* take place, and within a few days. Then his letter can be published with the maximum effect. This man is waging a campaign of terror, and he understands very well that nothing is so necessary as a fine sense of timing.'

'Come, Holmes!' I protested. 'You are surely overlooking the fact that the writer of this letter is a crude and simple fellow. You are making him out a man of intelligence and sophistication, when he is all too evidently a vulgar and illiterate ruffian.'

'You speak more wisely than you know, Watson. "All too evidently", indeed! Now I dare say I know more vulgar and illiterate ruffians than you, and I can assure you that none of them would perpetrate such a concoction as this. On the contrary, it is a characteristic of that type that, since writing is unnatural to them, they do it unnaturally. Their style is invariably cramped, their diction arch and stiff. But our correspondent who signs himself Jack the Ripper is quite a different sort. He uses his cant and his solecisms to achieve an effect, as though he were writing advertisements for the latest brand of liver pills. To be sure, he wishes the public to picture him as a violent low-class tough, which merely strengthens my conviction that he is in fact a gentleman; well spoken, well dressed, and quite probably eminently respected by a wide circle of acquaintances.'

Lestrade eyed me silently, and winked. It was only with difficulty that I refrained from returning the gesture. Holmes's description was so totally contrary to every current opinion—as well as to ordinary common sense—that I could not help wondering if he were indulging himself in a joke at our expense. But his features betrayed no hint of irony. He seemed, indeed, more than usually serious.

'Evidence!' he cried. 'That's what I need—evidence! Not the evidence he chooses to give out in his letter, nor what is left after a horde of the morbidly curious have trampled over the scene of the crime at sixpence a head. No, if our man is successful in carrying out this threat, I must be on the spot.'

He turned to Lestrade.

'What preventive measures are you contemplating?'

'Measures? Why, every spare man on the force has been drafted into Whitechapel! My only worry is that the killer will see that we've made the district too hot to hold him, and go somewhere else. If he was to try his luck in Bethnal Green or Stepney he might go many a mile without seeing a policeman.'

'Pshaw! Your fears are quite groundless, Lestrade. All the murderer's tactics so far have been expressly designed to create a confrontation between himself and the authorities—a confrontation he intends to win. Why else would he alert you to his intentions? To go elsewhere now would be tantamount to admitting defeat. Besides, it is obvious from his letter that he shares the low opinion of the force that is so sadly prevalent these days.'

'He will find a very warm welcome awaiting him if he does come back, I can promise you that,' Lestrade averred stoutly. 'Quite apart from our own patrols, and those of the vigilante groups, we have a little surprise up our sleeves. If the killer isn't very careful, he may well find that he has picked one of my constables to try and assault!'

'One of your constables?'

'That's what I said, Mr Holmes. This is highly confidential, of course, but you may be interested to learn that each night a body of our finest men patrol the streets of Whitechapel in female attire as decoys to trap this maniac.'

A moment of strained silence followed this revelation, and then Holmes and I burst simultaneously into uncontrollable laughter. Lestrade coloured deeply.

'I don't see anything funny!' he snapped. 'When it is a question of protecting the public and of apprehending criminals, I am proud to say that there are no lengths to which the Metropolitan Police are not prepared to go.'

'My dear fellow, you must excuse us,' cried Holmes. 'I feel sure I speak for Dr Watson in saying that I have nothing but the highest regard for the courage and devotion of your colleagues. It is just, you know, that the idea of our brawny and hirsute bobbies got up in linsey skirts and velvet bonnets takes a little getting used to.'

Lestrade's face was a picture of injured righteousness.

'It seems there's no pleasing you, Mr Holmes. You never tire of criticising us for doing things by the book, but as soon as we try something out of the ordinary you laugh in our faces. Well, I have more pressing business than to sit here joking with you two gentlemen. If I had known you weren't interested in working with us on this case, I wouldn't have troubled you.'

He got to his feet. Holmes also rose.

'You are quite mistaken if you think I am uninterested in the case, Inspector,' he said soothingly. 'On the contrary, nothing would give me greater pleasure than to be associated with your investigation. As I have said, I think it most likely that the murderer will attempt to strike within the next few nights. It is therefore imperative that our plans should be laid. If it is convenient, I propose we meet this afternoon at the Yard to discuss our strategy.'

Suitably mollified by this overture, Lestrade left in much better humour. Holmes saw him out, returning to the room with an expression of great glee.

'What a tonic our good Lestrade is, to be sure!' he cried. 'Believe me, Watson, if you ever feel that you are growing old and stupid, the best cure I know is the company of one of Her Majesty's detectives. They really should be hired out by the hour so that doctors could prescribe the remedy.'

'Surely you are a little harsh,' I objected. 'The authorities seem to me to have done everything that can be expected.'

'Exactly, my dear fellow! That's what I find so amusing. They do just what one expects, like so many clockwork toys. I must admit, though, that this latest stroke of Lestrade's is something I had not foreseen. Policemen in petticoats! I certainly hope they have their wits about them, or before long the illustrated papers may be proclaiming the discovery of the horribly mutilated body of a policeman dressed in whore's rags in a Spitalfields alley. Imagine that, Watson!'

I could not but deplore this banter, and I sought to turn the conversation to more seemly courses.

'Come now, Holmes! You rally the authorities freely enough, but what is your own solution? You refuse to give even a hint of daylight, yet you mock others for blundering in the dark. That's hardly sporting, you know.'

'Well said, old friend! No doubt I have been liberal with my jibes, and it is true I have no more idea of the murderer's identity than Lestrade does. But I do at least have a clear idea of what kind of man he is.'

'Here is a beast, a savage. That much is plain enough.'

Holmes glanced at me keenly.

'I believe that you have a theory, Doctor. Out with it, then! It is a free-for-all at this stage.'

'All right, then. I believe that the murderer of these poor women is some brutal savage like Tonga.* I note that the killings have all occurred close to the docks. Suppose that this native is employed as a deckhand on some foreign ship. Fresh from his barbarous homeland, he is set loose in London. Crazed with drink, he roams the streets by night. Then, chancing upon some penniless unfortunate huddled in a doorway, he kills her in his savage frenzy. He then slips back on board his ship, which sails at first light. His tracks are thus effectively covered, and when the vessel returns a few weeks later he is free to indulge in another bloodbath.'

Holmes applauded enthusiastically. 'Capital, Doctor! Really first rate! If I were in the market for a theory, I would sooner take yours than half a dozen others I have heard. In fact there is still more evidence you might adduce in its favour. The arrangement of the objects around Chapman's body, for instance, might be explained as a heathen rite.'

'I know nothing of that.'

'The killer took the rings from her fingers and laid them out carefully at her feet, together with a few coins. By her head he placed part of an envelope, and you have heard Dr Philips's evidence about the arrangement of the intestines on her right shoulder. Does that not suggest some form of ritual sacrifice?'

I could scarcely believe my ears. With each new detail the case seemed to grow darker and more unfathomable.

'It's devilish,' I cried.

'It has certainly been made to appear so. Incidentally, one of the inmates of the boarding-house Chapman frequented identified the envelope as being the property of the deceased. She had seen her with it earlier that night, but at that time it lacked the mark it bore later, when it was found by Chapman's head.'

'What mark was that?'

*Tonga, the Andaman Islander and bosom companion of Jonathan Small, features prominently in 'The Sign of Four'.

'The letter "M". A capital "M". That would seem to put paid to your ignoble savage, Watson.'

'Perhaps one of his fellow-seamen had taught him a few letters,' I suggested feebly. 'Or perhaps—'

My voice died away. Holmes nodded.

'Aye, "perhaps". There you have the key to this whole affair. "Perhaps." Have you ever heard of Occam's Razor?'

'What?' I was rather startled by this sudden change of tack. 'I don't believe I have. Is it one of the new safety models?'

'Hardly. It has been with us for over five hundred years. It is a philosophical axiom. In its original form it runs: *Entia non sunt multiplicanda.*'

'I see.'

'In other words, entities should not be unnecessarily multiplied. Now then, Doctor! How many theories are necessary to solve a problem?'

I sat up straight and endeavoured to collect my thoughts.

'How many are necessary? Well, just one. As long as it's the correct one, of course.'

'Precisely! But when we come to look into these Whitechapel murders, what do we find? Handfuls of theories! Theories by the score! One penny plain and tuppence coloured! Every man you meet has his own and every hour brings with it a fresh one. So let us try all these prolific hypotheses upon old William of Occam's cutting edge. Are they necessary to explain the facts? They are not. Do they bring us any nearer to apprehending the criminal? They do not. Do they enable us to predict what he is likely to do in the future? No. Then what use are they? The answer, my dear Watson, is that they are of no use whatsoever to us, but of very great value to the murderer.'

As Holmes expounded his argument, his tone grew more heated and his gestures correspondingly more intense. At length he leapt up from his chair and began to pace the floor.

'I said that I had a clear idea of the kind of man he

is, Watson. Perhaps now you begin to perceive the outlines. You must put all conventional notions out of your head. We are dealing with an artist of misdirection with an uncanny knack for manipulating the public mind. He knows that organ as well as any great musician knows his instrument, and he can make it play whatever medley of popular airs will best enshroud the augmented tones of his grim *leitmotif*. Is it any wonder then that Lestrade and company provoke my mirth? This Whitechapel killer is as far beyond their ken as Lassus's polyphony is beyond the patrons of the Savoy Theatre. In fact, Watson—and I say this without the slightest immodesty—I very much doubt whether there is any man in London besides myself who is capable of cutting through this cunning devil's webs of deception, to reveal the unholy genius at the heart of it all. He is truly a formidable opponent! Finally I have an adversary wholly worthy of my powers! To destroy him will set a fitting crown upon my life's work. And if I fail—But no! I must not fail. There can be no question of that! The consequences would be unthinkable.'

Never had I seen Holmes display such agitation as in uttering these last words. It was as if he found himself doubting his own powers for the first time. In another moment he was master of himself again, and all purposeful energy, but that single glimpse of the inner man disturbed me far more than all the dreadful news I had heard that morning.

Holmes spent the afternoon at Scotland Yard, returning for dinner in a mood of taciturn introspection. After the meal, which we ate in silence, he retired to the acid-stained table in the corner and busied himself with his retorts and test-tubes. I took myself out for a walk, and went early to bed. The next morning our front room reeked of some malodorous compound which Holmes had brewed up in what had evidently been a late sitting. Of Holmes himself there was no sign until almost midday, when he emerged from his room dressed as the shabbiest tatterdemalion imaginable, and announced coolly that he would spend the next three days in White-chapel.

'You mean to leave me behind then?' I cried in dismay.

'No, no. But you cannot assist me at this juncture. Fear not, though, you shall miss none of the sport.'

'Might I not at least tag along?'

'Tut, Watson! It wouldn't do, old fellow. I shall spend my time mingling with the people of the district. As you see, I intend to pass as one of themselves. Now I think you would agree that your dramatic talents do not extend much beyond the occasional recitation of "The boy stood on the burning deck" at yuletide festivities, whereas I must come and go in houses which the police themselves will not enter. If the folk there suspected for an instant that I was a "toff" I should be in great danger of leaving the premises horizontally.'

'That's all very well, Holmes, but you cannot expect me to sit idly by while you battle this fiend alone!'

'By no means. On the contrary, if things turn out as I expect I shall be only too glad of your support. As you know, I maintain a number of small refuges in various parts of London, and one of these is situated quite conveniently close to the scene of these crimes. I intend to put up there. It is too small to accommodate us both—a mere glory-hole—but Lestrade is to call for me if a murder is discovered, and I shall at once dispatch a cab to bring you to the spot.'

They also serve, the poem says, who only stand and wait. Perhaps their service is in fact the more arduous. Certainly it seemed so that evening as I sat alone in Baker Street, gazing into the fire and wondering what Holmes was about and what hazards he was facing and what the outcome would be. At eleven o'clock I lit my candle and went upstairs. I lay down fully clothed on my bed, and after a time sleep claimed me.

At half past two a rapping at my bedroom door awoke me from a fitful slumber. I was grateful for the interruption, for I had been visited by a fantastic and terrible dream in which I seemed to be following a woman down a dreary street, a knife in my hand. From such unwholesome phantoms even the rudest awakening comes as a welcome relief. At the door I discovered Mrs Hudson's Billy, clad in a woollen wrap and shaking with cold and excitement.

'There's a cab for you down below, sir,' said the youth. 'Mr Holmes 'as sent for you, seein' as which there's bin another 'orrible murder!'

The situation had proved too much for Billy's grammar, but his meaning could not have been clearer. I fetched my hat and coat and hurried down. But it soon seemed that I had shaken off my dreams only to enter a world equally spectral and oppressive. The hansom bucked and swayed through deserted streets. A chill wind had laid waste the city. How many of all the millions who toil daily in London have ever seen its other face? It is an eerie reflection of that brash and bustling metropolis. All is the same, and yet not the same. No doubt it sounds fanciful, but seen from that madly dashing cab the city bore the aspect of a skull. The very streets seemed terrible, and a fit arena for these most terrible crimes.

The cabbie had said only that the murder was in Aldgate. 'They wouldn't let me near the body. They said it was no fit sight.' We sped down Holborn and Cheapside, past the Bank, and into Leadenhall Street. Here at last the driver checked our furious progress, as we turned off down a narrow lane to the left. Some distance along we turned again, and drew up. The cabbie jumped down. 'You're here,' he said bluntly.

A cut opposite debouched into a small square where a group of persons were gathered together under a lamp. As I approached, a policeman emerged from the shadows and asked me my business. I explained that I was an associate of Mr Sherlock Holmes, upon which I was conducted to the group under the lamp and introduced to an Inspector of the City Police. This official denied all knowledge of Holmes's whereabouts, but on learning that I was a doctor he in turn introduced me to the police surgeon, a Dr Brown, who was waiting for arrangements to be made to remove the corpse to the mortuary. It was he who invited me to view the remains.

'I have no idea how extensive your practice has been, Dr Watson,' he remarked, 'but I shall be very surprised if you have seen anything like this before.'

He led me across the square to a dark corner. On the flagstones lay a shapeless mass. The surgeon shone his bull's-eye on it, and bent to turn back the sheet of dirty canvas that covered the thing. It was a dead woman. Her throat had been slashed in the most vicious manner, and the whole face was brutally disfigured. Pieces of bloody tissue were heaped about the neck. Then Dr Brown pulled the canvas all the way back, exposing the lower body to view.

For a moment I was in danger of disgracing myself before a fellow medico. And yet that corpse presented nothing new to eyes that had witnessed countless dissections. It was not the injuries themselves that were so shocking—the gaping abdomen, the entrails torn asunder, the pools of drying blood—but rather the terrible violence with which they had been inflicted. Nothing that was said at the inquest could begin to suggest the impression that was immediately burned upon the mind of everyone who saw that poor woman's body. The knife had been jabbed with tremendous force into the groin and then dragged upwards through the body until it was stopped by the breast-bone. The signature on the letter Lestrade had shown us leapt instantly to mind in all its hideous aptness—the woman had been literally ripped open. All those present that morning were either doctors or policemen, and by profession inured to grisly scenes, and yet they all conspicuously avoided the corner where the body lay, and huddled together on the other side of the square as if for protection. I knew that each man had felt as I had on gazing at that obscene spectacle, that some dark power had risen out of the swamps of history, some atavistic freak come to unleash horrors we had thought to meet only in old books and country tales, and with which we were helpless to deal.

Brown covered the body again, and we rejoined the others. After a time I fell in conversation with the constable who had discovered the crime. He told me that he had passed through the square on his rounds at half past one, and had seen nothing untoward.

'Fifteen minutes later I came through again, and there she was,' the fellow declared solemnly. 'I've been on the force a few years now, but I've never seen nothing like that. I hope to God I never shall again! There she was, just like you saw her, laying on her back with her skirts hoisted up and her legs spread and all her guts hanging out. It can't help but give you a bit of a turn, you know, coming on the likes of that without fair warning. Anyway, I ran over here to the warehouse, and the watchman went off to fetch some others while I stayed with the body. Then later the Commissioner comes round in a cab, and I showed her to him myself.'*

By now I was feeling increasingly concerned by Holmes's continuing absence. How comforting it would be to watch him at work, evaluating the evidence that others had overlooked, forming and testing theories, dropping sibylline remarks or stubbornly keeping his own counsel. At his side, I knew, the terror that had possessed my soul would recede and diminish, until at last this abomination would come to seem natural and explicable and its author an ordinary mortal like ourselves. When the constable had concluded his account, therefore, I asked him whether he had seen my friend. Much to my surprise he answered readily:

'Mr Holmes, sir? Why yes! He was here not long after Sir Henry. About a quarter past two it must have been. There was a little foxy-looking fellow with him. An Inspector from the Yard, he said.'

'That would be Lestrade,' I confirmed.

'Yes, sir, that was his name. They were come straight from the other murder, and when—'

---

*The 'Commissioner' referred to is Lieutenant-Colonel Sir Henry Smith, then Acting Commissioner of the City of London Police.

'What! The other murder! You mean there has been another atrocity tonight?'

'Why yes, sir, Have you not heard? There's another woman killed, down the Commercial Road East. Her throat was cut the same as this one, like he had a mind to take her head home with him. He did that one before, though. Around one o'clock they found her, and then when they got news of this one they came straight over.'

'But they are not here now?'

'Oh no, sir! They didn't stop long. First Mr Holmes had a look at the body, then he whips out this magnifying-glass, goes down on all fours and starts crawling about the square. The gent from the Yard stands here watching with what you might call a smirk. All of a sudden Mr Holmes jumps up. "This way!" he calls out, and they went off through that cut over there.'

The man pointed to a narrow passage at the end of the square. I was just wondering whether I should go that way myself, in hopes of finding Holmes, when I heard a clatter of hoofs and the scraping of a wheel against the kerb. With mingled pleasure and relief I heard my friend's voice hailing me. I hurried over to the waiting hansom. Holmes opened the doors and helped me up.

'Goulston Street, cabbie!' he called out, and we drove off. 'He has escaped us, Watson! We had him in our net, but somehow he has given us the slip. We followed his trail as far as Dorset Street, but there we lost him. Lestrade is busy turning out all the doss-houses in the area.'

'He may yet be apprehended, then!'

'I think not. Such a refuge would be too public to suit our man's requirements. Lestrade will almost certainly achieve nothing more than waking up a large number of exhausted paupers. No, I fear the killer has got clean away this time. There is nothing more we can do here. I just want to show you something of interest, and then we may go home.'

His voice was lifeless and his whole bearing weary

and dispirited. After a short journey the cab drew up in a gloomy and forbidding street composed of tall dwelling-houses built to a common model. Holmes bade the driver wait, and led me to the entrance of one of the buildings, where a sturdy man in an ulster was standing. Holmes greeted him.

'Well, Halse, anything new? Are they still set on rubbing it off?'

'So it seems, Mr Holmes. I've sent for a photographer, but we can do nothing until it gets light. It seems the Yard is still worried there might be a riot if the writing is seen.'

'I should have thought Warren would have seen all in favour of that,' Holmes returned drily. 'Putting down riots is his *forte*, isn't it?'*

Halse smothered a grin.

'All I know is if we were standing on the other side of Petticoat Lane, this business would be handled differently. But this is Metropolitan ground, and they've got an Inspector in there with a bath sponge waiting to wipe off the writing the moment a crowd gathers. They call it maintaining the peace. I won't tell you what I call it.'

At this point I could restrain myself no longer.

'What writing are you talking about? What has happened?'

Holmes turned to me apologetically.

'My dear fellow, do forgive me. I had quite forgotten that you are not yet *au courant*. This is Detective Sergeant Halse of the City Police, who is keeping an unofficial eye this being outside his bailiwick—on the imbeciles from Scotland Yard, who seem bent on erasing one of the most interesting clues we have in this affair. Look over here!'

Taking a lantern from the policeman, Holmes illuminated a portion of the wall at the entrance to the build-

*Sir Charles Warren was Commissioner of the Metropolitan Police. His peremptory handling of a procession and demonstration by the Radical and Socialist Clubs the previous year had resulted in the Trafalgar Square riots (13 November 1887) and aroused much adverse criticism.

ing. Some words were scrawled there in chalk on the black dado.

> The Juwes are
> The men That
>         Will not
> be Blamed
>         for nothing

'An interesting example of killer's graffiti, is it not?' commented Holmes.

'But how can you tell he did it? It could have been put there by almost anyone.'

Holmes shook his head decisively.

'Note the long strokes on the "t"s, the slope of the double "l"s, the almost separated "m"s and the oval "o"s. Altogether there are some seventeen quite unmistakable correspondences with the letter Lestrade showed us on Friday. But we have more conclusive proof. A piece of bloodstained cloth was found with the writing, and there is no doubt that it was cut from the apron of the woman whose remains you just inspected in Mitre Square. He used it to wipe his hands on before penning these lines.'

'My God!'

'Quite. Well, so much for that. Nothing now remains but to return to Baker Street and put our brains to work. Good night, Halse. Try and save us from our friends.'

'I will do what I can, Mr Holmes.'

As we drove back across that unpatrolled frontier which separates the territories of the two great tribes which inhabit London, Holmes maintained his dour and troubled silence. I could tell that he was goading himself with recriminations and reproaches—as if any man could have succeeded where he had failed—and I thought it best to interrupt this morbid introspection.

'I say, Holmes, you might tell me what has happened tonight, you know! I'm still pretty much in the dark.'

'Of course, of course. I may as well recount my experiences in the order in which they occurred. I reached my retreat shortly after ten, and passed a few hours with a pipe and my pocket Seneca before retiring. Lestrade's man roused me at ten minutes before two. The body of the first victim had been found an hour before, in a courtyard off Berner Street, by a hawker returning from Sydenham market. The police were summoned. Lestrade, who was at Leman Street station, was notified, and as soon as he had verified that it was indeed another Ripper murder, he sent for me.'

'Verified? But how could there be any question? Is it possible to have the slightest doubt whose hand inflicted those dreadful mutilations?'

Holmes wagged his forefinger at me.

'Ah! Therein lies the interest of the Berner Street killing. The body was not mutilated.'

'It was not?'

'Not in any way.'

'Then how did you know—'

'Because of the way the throat had been cut. And because of what happened forty minutes later in Mitre Square.'

In a flash I perceived the fearful pattern.

'The second woman was killed because he had been unable to mutilate the first?'

'Precisely. The Berner Street victim was still warm when discovered. The blood was flowing from the throat. She can have been dead no more than a few minutes. The murderer was in fact probably still in the yard.'

'He was still there?'

'I am certain of it. Why should he have left? Put yourself in his shoes for a moment. You have just killed your intended victim and are about to butcher her— such butchery being the object of the exercise—when you hear a pony-trap coming along the street. It is a hundred to one against it turning in, so you retire into the shadows, confident of being able to resume your work immediately. But instead of passing by, the cart pulls into the yard. The horse shies at the smell of blood, and the driver gets down to investigate. At that point, of course, you realise that the game is up, and slip away while the man is fumbling for his matches.'

'You must be right, Holmes,' I declared. 'No doubt the murderer was hiding close by. How infuriating! If only he had been spotted! His luck is devilish.'

'I doubt very much whether he would have agreed with you,' Holmes retorted. 'Consider the position in which he now found himself. Here is a man who has deliberately set out to appal the civilised world with abominations of such enormity that the details cannot even be set forth in print. No one knows better than he how needful it is to maintain the crescendo of horror. It is no good falling back on mere throat-cutting when his public has come to expect evisceration. There is therefore but one course open to him—another killing, *instanter,* and this time followed by the most thorough disembowelment of the victim.'

I shook my head in amazement at this extraordinary series of events.

'Strange indeed are the ways of fate,' I remarked. 'Had that hawker only been delayed a few minutes, that poor woman I saw would still be alive and whole.'

'No doubt, but the argument is puerile,' Holmes replied severely. 'Let us abstain from fruitless conjecture and devote our energies to an analysis of the known facts. Now we know that on leaving Berner Street the murderer walked west—'

'I don't see what evidence there is for that,' I returned somewhat peevishly. 'As you said, forty minutes elapsed before the next killing. He might have gone a longer route and still reached Mitre Square in good time. Surely it is in fact most likely that he went north to Spitalfields in search of another victim. They were saying at the club that the area is one of the best, I mean the worst, in that respect.'

'Dear me, Watson, have you been at my cocaine by any chance? You coruscate this morning! But here we are in Baker Street. Let us postpone this most interesting discussion for a few minutes. Thank you cabbie, this will do.'

Once in our rooms, Holmes threw himself down in his wonted chair and lit his cherry-wood pipe.

'Perhaps you would rather turn in, Watson? It has been a long night.'

'I am quite awake now.'

'You were asking, I believe, how we can know that the killer did not solicit his victim in Spitalfields. The answer is simple. She was not in Spitalfields. Until one o'clock this morning she was in Bishopsgate police station under lock and key.'

'Good heavens!'

'One of the constables who were called to Mitre Square when the body was discovered remembered having spoken to her during the time she was in custody. She had been taken in charge earlier in the evening as drunk and incapable. Incidentally, if you still wish to indulge in idle speculation, you might care to consider the fact that had the woman chosen to get drunk in Whitechapel rather than in Aldgate she would not now be forming the subject of our conversation.'

'The murderer would not have met her, you mean?'

'Not unless he was arrested himself, and put in the same cell. In Whitechapel, you see, she would have been apprehended by the Metropolitan Police, whose Commissioner, Warren, is a teetotaller who insists on the letter of the law. The woman would have spent the night in the cells, to be haled before a magistrate in the morning. The City Police, on the other hand, are in the habit of releasing any revellers who have sobered up sufficiently by one o'clock in the morning. Kate Kelly, which was the name she gave, was duly inspected at that hour and found to be presentable. Thus at the very moment that the costermonger was frustrating the Ripper in Berner Street, his next victim was being set free less than a mile away in the City. For the next twenty minutes or so each proceeded, all unknowing, towards the other.'

Holmes fell silent. It seemed as though even his coldly rational mind had been overcome by the sensation of an implacable fate permeating every aspect of these dreadful crimes. We both sat staring into the cold ashes in the grate, no doubt sharing the same thoughts, but both unwilling to voice them for fear of ridicule. What impressed me above all was how everything conspired to further the murderer's schemes. He was always at the right place at the right time, his prey close to hand, whilst his pursuers could do no more than trace the trail of gore and say, 'He has been here, and here.'

At length I rose, hoping to lose these gloomy notions in sleep. Holmes bade me a subdued good night, and I made my way upstairs to bed once more. But there too I could think of nothing but the violated body of that pathetic old woman. The image loomed up in the darkness on every side. Finally the light of dawn dissolved the screen on which the horrid peep-show was displayed, and I slept.

# *Two*

If this narrative of mine tends to substantiate the old adage that fact is stranger than fiction, it also demonstrates how very much less well-ordered it is. If this were one of A.C.D.'s tales you may be sure the action would follow fast and furious. If my notes showed that such-and-such a case took three months to complete, why! a slip of the pen would make it three days, and a much more satisfying story. But this is not a story, and I do not undertake to satisfy those seeking light relief from their daily cares. I must therefore record that during the two weeks immediately following the events just described, Holmes and I had nothing more to do with the mystery of the Whitechapel murderer. The reason, to quote another proverb, is that it never rains but it pours. From the 2nd until the 12th of October, Holmes was unexpectedly occupied with two brief and perhaps rather superficial cases. These were, respectively, the circumstances surrounding the disappearance and recovery of the famous racehorse Silver Blaze, and the bizarre business of Lord Robert St Simon's illusory wedding. A.C.D. later included both cases in his collection of stories based on my notes, and since the events are in any case quite extraneous to my present purpose I do not propose to dwell on them any further.

I have said that during this period Holmes and I had nothing more to do with the Ripper murders, but this statement demands qualification. Hardly a literate person in the country, and certainly no devourer of newsprint as voracious as Holmes, could have remained unconscious of every new development in the case, whether substantial or merely sensational. Whatever they may have been to the people of London, the events of the 30th of September were a godsend to the press. Periodicals notorious for their ailing circulations, including several long given up as hopeless by their financial advisers, suddenly sprang to life with special editions which were snatched from the presses and eagerly perused before the ink was well dry. And should a copy or two remain unaccountably on their hands, the newsboys had only to holler, 'Murder, Ghastly, Horrible, Mutilations, Terrible,' etc., and in the twinkling of an eye their stock would be exhausted.

The inquests on the two women were reported in lurid detail. The leading articles severely criticised the police for their incompetence, while in the correspondence columns theories as to the murderer's motives and identity were heatedly debated. Respectable gentlemen living in sedate suburbs offered their services to the authorities, who were already inundated with letters accusing the writer's friends and relations, or merely issuing illiterate and often illegible threats. This last class were for the most part blatant plagiarisms of the letter signed 'Jack the Ripper', of which the authorities had issued a reproduction in the form of a poster. Following the inquests, the witnesses' depositions were checked and compared, and three dissimilar descriptions of the wanted man were issued. A reward of £500 was even offered for information leading to his arrest. But all the trails proved false, all the openings blind alleys, and every clue circular and ambiguous. The public mood was an ugly mixture of hatred and terror that was very close to panic.

To outward appearances, Holmes was totally absorbed all this time by the two cases to which I referred, but it was clear to me that his energies were by no means wholly engaged by the problems they presented. One might liken his mood to that of an artist who pauses during the creation of some vast epic canvas to paint a pair of portraits—light, straightforward, employing only his superb technical skill—while his spirit rests from its intense labours and prepares for renewed struggle. On several occasions he brought up the subject of the double murder, which clearly continued to occupy his thoughts. Thus my notes reveal that at breakfast on Friday the 5th, following our return from Dartmoor on the night express,* Holmes looked up from his paper with a triumphant air.

"Ha! She was going to Bermondsey, Watson.'

'What? Who?'

'Catherine Eddowes, alias Kate Kelly—the Mitre Square victim. I always wondered why she did not go home to her lodging-house in Fashion Street when they

---

*King's Pyland stables on Dartmoor was the scene of the disappearance of Silver Blaze.

released her. She was seen to go off down Houndsditch, you know. Why?'

'Does it matter, Holmes?' I enquired grumpily. I tend to be a trifle sullen first thing in the morning, and nothing is less congenial at such times than vigorous interrogation.

'Of course it matters! Everything matters in a case as obscure as this. That is, Doctor, unless you are possessed of some private knowledge which allows you to determine what is material and what is not?'

I was silent, studying the interior of my egg.

'My provisional theory', continued Holmes in his earlier discursive tone, 'was that she was going down to the Minories to recoup her finances in the way she knew best. But according to her male companion, one John Kelly, she had a daughter living in Bermondsey from whom she had spoken earlier on the Saturday of borrowing some money. She was no doubt bound thither when she met up with the killer.'

I felt obliged to make some comment.

'What puzzles me is why the murderer was in such a hurry. Why did he not return to his lair and clean himself up instead of dashing round the streets with bloody hands? He seems to have taken incredible risks for no very good reason.'

'His reason was the best in the world,' cried Holmes. 'He had been foiled, don't you see? This Jew Diemschutz, this common costermonger, had interfered with his grand designs. He must have been seething with fury as he stalked off in search of a substitute victim. He had to show the police and the public—and himself—that he was still the same supernatural and impersonal force which the press has made him appear. He had to demonstrate conclusively that his will cannot be thwarted for more than a few minutes. How he must have fretted over his rebuff! How he must have burned to avenge it! You saw the result.'

Once again I was forced to marvel at Holmes's ability to penetrate to the core of the mystery, and to unravel the twisted strands of the murderer's character.

As I mentioned above, the authorities issued posters in the wake of the killings, printing a facsimile of the letter Lestrade had shown us together with a postcard in the same hand which had been received at the Central News Agency the day after the murders. A superscription requested any person recognising the writing to communicate with the police. Lestrade deposited a copy of the poster at 221B during a visit in connection with the St Simon affair. I still have it, more than forty years after. The letter I have already transcribed. The card, which was badly smeared with blood, ran this way:

> I was not codding dear old Boss when I gave you the tip. youll hear about saucy Jackys work tomorrow. double event this time　　number one squealed a bit couldnt finish straight off.　　had no time to get ears for police　　thanks for keeping last letter back till I got to work again.
>
> 　　　　　　　　　　　　　　　　Jack the Ripper

Holmes wrenched the knife which secured his unanswered correspondence from the mantelpiece, and then drove it angrily back into the wood.

' "Dear old Boss"!' he snapped. ' "Saucy Jacky"! What sickening cant! And what a loathsome miscarriage of genius lies behind it all! I tell you, Watson, just thinking about this man makes me feel queasy. I would to God I might face an army of Grimesby Roylotts rather than spend another instant in the intellectual company of this pollution.'

It occurred to me that the murderer's reference to his attempt to cut off the woman's ears suggested a parallel with the Cushing case, but I said nothing. In his present mood, Holmes would probably have replied with some crushing sarcasm to the effect that I at least always managed to keep my feet flat on the ground; just as, at another time, had I been guilty of his late outburst, he would have been quite capable of telling me curtly to cut out the emotional gush and stick to the facts. Living with great men is itself a minor art.

On Friday the 12th of October, Holmes introduced Mr and Mrs Francis Hay Moulton to Lord Robert St Simon, thereby bringing to an end his investigation of what A.C.D. was to call the adventure of 'The Noble Bachelor'. For the following week I saw very little of my friend. After a day or two of being scowled at whenever I entered the room, and then treated to encomiums on the excellence of the autumn air and references to how much my fellow-members at the club must be missing me, I took the point and left Holmes to his own devices. These proved exceedingly singular. My glimpses of Holmes were few and far between, but each was memorable. One evening I would return home to discover him seated Buddha-like on the floor, his eyes fixed unseeingly before him and the air dark with the highly unexotic incense of smouldering shag. The following day there would be no sign of him, but next morning he would burst in as I was breakfasting, attired as a sewer scavenger, complete with noxious stench.* The day after that I had barely turned out of George Street when I heard what sounded like a madman playing a fiddle. As I neared Number 221, I realised that the noise was emanating from our rooms, where Holmes was scraping out the same dozen notes over and over again, creating a terrible cacophony devoid of either harmony or rhythm. On Tuesday I found him kneeling on the rug in the front room, slashing the body of a suckling pig with a knife from his old medical kit, and then examining the resulting incisions minutely through his magnifying-glass. Mrs Hudson roasted the pig the next evening, but I was obliged to dine alone, since Holmes had not returned from the sortie he had made that morning in the character of an officer of the Salvation Army.

At last, one Saturday morning, the fit left him and life returned to what passed for normality at 221B

*Sewer scavengers, or toshers, made their living by entering the London sewer system and sieving for items of value. Those who survived the tides and the rats could make as much as £2 a week.

Baker Street. I came down to find my friend already savouring his pipe and leafing through the papers. I greeted him minimally and rang for my breakfast.

'So, my dear Doctor,' exclaimed Holmes from behind *The Times,* 'whilst I wear myself out combing London for a murderer, you spend your nights dining off Simpson's beef and quaffing the Beaune of a comet year.'

I started guiltily.

'Pray how goes it with young Stamford?' Holmes continued evenly.

'Stamford? But—But my dear Holmes! This is incredible!'

'Pooh! Elementary, my boy. *Primo*: our landlady informed me last night that you had wired from your club to tell her you would not be home to dinner. *Secondo*: that piece of paper, which you placed on the mantelpiece last night, bears an address in Pinner and a large wine-stain. *Tertio*: your boots have been set out to dry in plain view. You are well acquainted with my methods, so naturally I need not explain the absurdly simple argument leading from this trio of facts to my conclusion. Need I?'

'Well—'

'Oh very well then. When a man of your admirable regularity of character decides at the last moment that he will dine from home, we may confidently assume that he has unexpectedly met an acquaintance. In the present case we may further assume that this meeting occurred at your club, since it was from there that you dispatched the telegram. The question therefore becomes: whom might you run into at the club who could induce you to forgo Mrs Hudson's inimitable cuisine? You will see at once that the answer can only be young Stamford. You never cease harping on the unutterable dreariness of the other members, and only last month you were bemoaning the fact that Stamford's visits to the institution would now be few and far between, since he had just acquired a practice in Middlesex. What more likely, then, than that he should be spending the weekend in town, and that the two of you should repair to Simpson's for dinner, in the course of which you jotted down his new address? I fear the explanation is as tedious as it is unnecessary.'

By now I had recovered sufficiently to play my part.

'But how do you know we went to Simpson's?'

Holmes smiled indulgently.

'From your boots. And from that same regularity of character to which I have already alluded. My dear fellow, capriciousness is simply not one of your vices! You have but one newspaper, one club, one political party, one tobacco, and one tailor. Should you need to resort to a restaurant, you have but one, and it is Simpson's. My conviction on this point is merely corroborated by the unmistakable traces on your boots of an interesting argillaceous loam, large quantities of which are at present inconveniencing pedestrians in the Strand due to the roadworks.'

'Very well, Holmes, but the wine? You mean to tell me that you can tell one variety from another by studying the stain?'

'I have no doubt whatever that it would be possible, but I have not undertaken any research on the subject. The British criminal is not enough of a wine-bibber for it to pay dividends. But it would be folly to order anything but beef at Simpson's, and I happen to know that your gastronomical rule of thumb is "Beef on the bone, Beaune with the beef." '

'Amazing,' I muttered, and 'Wonderful,' but I was actually trembling with relief. I had indeed dined out the previous evening, but not with Stamford. My companion had been Mary Morstan. Our engagement was proving rather trying. Quite apart from various tedious financial questions on which I need not dwell, I was practically speaking in the position of a man maintaining two households. True, Holmes had retreated from the position of extreme displeasure which he had adopted on learning of my intention to wed. But the matter was never spoken of between us—indeed,

Mary's name was never mentioned. I felt there was a tacit agreement that the whole question of my nuptials should simply be ignored at 221B Baker Street, and that it was only on this understanding that I was to remain *persona grata* there. So whenever Mary and I wished to meet, I had to slip away secretly. On the Friday in question, tiring of visiting her in Camberwell, I had invited Mary and her friend Mrs Forrester to dine with me, but it was not until I was sipping a preprandial B. and S. at the club that I realised I had forgotten to inform Mrs Hudson of my intentions. Having sent my wire I strolled along the Strand to the Lyceum Theatre, whose portico Mary and I used as a trysting-place, for sentimental reasons.* The three of us then drove to a rather entertaining little place in Mayfair recommended by Mrs Forrester. The wine was Chianti and the address that of Miss Morstan's aunt, with whom she was to spend the weekend.

Having recounted one of Holmes's rare blunders, I should add that this sort of exercise was to him no more than a form of parlour-game. He was perfectly aware of the weakness of unsupported inference, and in any question of importance he used it merely as one weapon in his formidable intellectual armoury.

Normal relations having been resumed, Holmes proceeded to favour me with that mixture of ironic observations, gentle chaffing and pontifical dicta which made up his conversation. Evidently he was in good spirits, and I felt this must spell some success in his investigations. What this might be I knew he would reveal in his own good time, and I made no attempt to question him. Having finished my meal I went to the fireplace to light a cigarette. As I blew out the match I heard Holmes groan. I looked up at the mirror. He was standing at the bay-window, facing out. His figure rose tall and dark against the sunlight streaming into the room.

*The Lyceum—'third pillar from the left'—was the spot assigned by Thaddeus Sholto for Mary Morstan to meet his representative, thereby initiating the series of events which were to lead to Watson's engagement.

'What is it, Holmes? What's the matter?'

He whirled around towards me. His features, I noted with a thrill of horror, were ashen and drawn. I turned to face him, deeply shaken by this sudden crisis.

'Holmes!'

His look was one of sheer desperation. He spoke steadily enough, though I could see it cost him an effort.

'Can you spare an hour or so just now, Watson?'

'Of course, but—'

'Then get your hat and coat.'

A few minutes later we were walking briskly up Baker Street and into York Place. Whatever had so dramatically affected my friend had presumably been visible in the street, but the scene about us presented no sinister or unusual aspect to my eyes. Holmes strode straight ahead, as if blinkered. At the corner of the Marylebone Road this attitude led to a collision with a passer-by, as a result of which Holmes dropped his stick. As he bent to retrieve it I was truly astounded to hear him utter an oath.

'I say, Holmes! What on earth is—'

'Not a word, Watson! But if you love me, stick close!'

With that he rushed out into the street and hailed a passing cab.

'Paddington Station, driver, and there's a guinea for you if we are there in five minutes!'

Duly impressed, the jarvey cracked his whip and we sped away, soon merging into the streaming traffic of the great highway. But no sooner had we reached the Edgware Road than Holmes sprang to the trap.

'Driver! My friend was in error! The station we want is Euston! I'll double the guinea if you can get us there in time!'

The hansom swung smartly around in the teeth of the oncoming vehicles, and in another instant we were rattling back the way we had come. But if I thought that Holmes's repertoire of surprises was now exhausted, I was sadly mistaken. When we were better than half way to our destination, the cab happened to be held up for a moment by a blockage of traffic. With a cry of 'Come, Watson!' Holmes leapt into the road. Ignoring the cabbie's shouts, I followed suit, and after a narrow escape from being crushed under a brewer's dray I reached safety just in time to see my friend disappearing into the Portland Road railway station.* After thirty-five smelly and noisy minutes underground, we emerged into the light of day once more on the Embankment. Holmes now led me at an unrelenting pace through a maze of alleys and passages. We entered a prestigious hotel through the front door and left via the kitchens, and then reversed this procedure with an equally famous military club. After a long sequence of this feinting, we finally came to rest in the pastoral serenity of St James's Park.

If Holmes wished to calm his nerves and regain his composure, he could have chosen no more suitable place. St James's Park is, without doubt, the most reassuring place on earth to an Englishman. There one sits in what resembles nothing so much as a bigger and better garden of childhood, surrounded by ducks and trees and quiet walks, walled in by the massive edifices lining Whitehall and the Mall—and ever calmly conscious of the great house to the west, from which the Empire's supreme parent keeps watch over the doings of her scattered family.

'You are a stout fellow, Watson, and a true soldier,' said Holmes at last. 'Nothing is as valuable as a friend who is content to follow without asking the reason why. You realised, no doubt, that we were being dogged.'

'I thought as much. But by whom?'

'Can you not guess?'

'Not I.'

'His tradename, as he himself puts it, is Jack the Ripper.'

'Holmes!'

I was stunned. A hundred questions sprang up at

*Now Great Portland Street station, on the Metropolitan and Circle lines.

once in my mind, demanding answers. How had Holmes identified the killer? Who was he? Why had the police not been informed? What dire purpose had he in following us about London?'

'You saw him, then, through the window?'

'Exactly.'

'But where was he, Holmes?'

'Have you noticed that one of the houses almost opposite our rooms has been standing empty for some time? He was there, at the first-floor windows. I happened to glance over, and there stood the very man who was at that moment uppermost in my thoughts. It was, as you may imagine, an unpleasant surprise. He was watching our rooms, Watson! He must know that I am on his trail. It is a major setback. I had hoped to have the advantage of him—to know, and not be known. No doubt it was a vain hope with such a man. But I shall have to watch my step very carefully from now on. We are dealing with one of the three most dangerous criminals in Europe.'

'But who is he?' I broke out impatiently. 'Who is Jack the Ripper?'

Holmes was silent for a moment. Then he shot a glance at me.

'You have probably never heard of Professor Moriarty?'

'Never.'

'Aye, there's the genius and the wonder of the thing!' he laughed bitterly. 'The man pervades London, and no one has ever heard of him. That's what puts him on a pinnacle in the records of crime. In those annals, eminence is measured not by how many people are aware of one, but by how few. Notoriety is a sure sign of incompetence. It is a point which is generally missed by the public and the press alike. Mention great criminals and they think of such men as Palmer and Peace.* But Palmer and Peace were hanged. The truly great criminal

*William Palmer (1825–56), doctor and poisoner, and Charles Peace (1832–79), burglar and murderer.

remains unknown. His deeds float free of him, unat-
tached, like natural events. The perfect crime exists,
Watson, but a necessary concomitant of its perfection is
that we do not know who committed it. If we did, we
should recognise behind many perfect crimes the hand
of the perfect criminal—Professor Moriarty!'

'What has he done, then?'

'His career has been extraordinary. He is of good
birth and excellent education, endowed by Nature with
a phenomenal mathematical faculty. At the age of
twenty-one he wrote a treatise upon the Binomial Theo-
rem which has had a European vogue. On the strength
of it he won the Chair of Mathematics at one of our
smaller universities, and had, to all appearance, a brilliant future ahead of him. Then, quite abruptly, he resigned his post and vanished into a carefully cultivated
obscurity.'

Holmes paused, as if to marshal his thoughts into a
suitably cogent form. I waited in silence, knowing better
than to try and prompt him.

'For some years now,' he began, 'I have been conscious of some power behind the common criminal—
some complex organising intelligence. It revealed itself
in many ways, most of them seemingly insignificant, but
together forming a quite remarkable pattern. One would
come across a gang of low-class roughs executing a robbery which they could never have planned. A convicted
murderer, hours away from the hangman, steadfastly
refuses to yield up the information that would implicate
others, and his widow later receives a large sum from an
anonymous benefactor. Another criminal is induced to
"peach", and the whole gang is taken; not one escapes
the net, and yet the informer is found floating in the
Thames a few days later. As soon as I perceived this
pattern, and read its meaning, I bent all my energies in
the attempt to identify and bring to justice the mysterious agent behind these diverse effects. Only then did I
appreciate the skill with which he had woven his web. It
is a masterpiece of duplicity, Watson! He has created a
nightmare world that parallels our own, but where paths

lead nowhere, words mean nothing, and no one is what he appears! Do what I would, I could not get the evidence to convict the Professor in a court of law. You know my powers, and yet in this man I had to acknowledge my intellectual equal. My horror at his crimes was lost in my admiration at his skill.

'Then, two months ago, the situation changed once again. As abruptly as he had withdrawn from academe, Moriarty now withdrew from the London underworld. You are aware of course that no one knows that world as I do, and at the beginning of August I became conscious of a great absence. The guiding hand was gone, and the machine it had built was falling asunder. Moriarty had wound up his operation and had once again disappeared from view. His house stood untenanted; his associates dispersed; chaos and old night descended once more upon the criminal scene. I was mystified. Nothing in the Professor's nefarious career puzzled me so much as his abandoning it at the height of his success, unthreatened even by me. It seemed completely inexplicable. Here in London the richest pickings in the world were his. "What a place to plunder!" the Prussian said,* and Moriarty had taken him at his word. No other scene could have offered him more. What, then, had become of him?'

'I suppose he might have been taking a holiday. August is the traditional month, after all.'

Holmes stared at me intently for a moment.

'Watson', he said quietly, 'I never get your limits. Never.'

I glowed with pleasure at this unwonted praise. Holmes looked around us on all sides before continuing, but the park was deserted.

'As I was saying, Moriarty's absence puzzled me sorely. Then these murders intervened, and I had other things to think about. It was only recently that I began

---

*Field-marshal Gebhard Leberecht von Blücher (1742–1819). The remark was allegedly made during a visit to London in 1814.

to consider the possibility that these two mysteries might be connected.'

Flushed with my earlier success, I spoke up again.

'But surely that should have been obvious, Holmes. Moriarty vanished in August—the very same month that these terrible killings started. I would have thought that—'

'No, Watson, it was not obvious!' Holmes's tone was sternly reproving. 'Moriarty, as you perhaps heard me say, was an organiser merely. He was, so to speak, the Napoleon of crime. You do not expect to find Napoleon leaving his maps and spy-glass to carry a sabre in the line. Moriarty was a man who acted indirectly for the purpose of gaining power and wealth. The Whitechapel killer acts in the most direct manner imaginable, but for no apparent purpose whatsoever. The two cases could hardly be more sharply contrasted.'

'Then why—? I mean, how—'

'Not so obvious now, eh Watson? Nevertheless, I think we can arrive at a fairly accurate notion of what it is that has induced this Bonaparte to start ripping flesh apart. Consider his university career. There, too, he found himself in an unrivalled position, enjoying an absolute and unclouded success. To be sure, various dark rumours circulated at the time of his resignation, but I have been able to show that these were started by none other than the Professor himself, as a smoke-screen to cover his withdrawal. We are therefore forced to the conclusion that there is something in Moriarty's disposition which abhors absolute and unclouded success. He has a strain in his blood which craves challenge as other men crave drugs. No sooner has he mastered a profession than he abandons it in disgust. His book *The Dynamics of an Asteroid* was so abstruse that no one could be found who was competent to offer an opinion upon it. Thereupon, he turned his hand to crime. But here again he soon proved himself *hors concours*. Even I, the foremost criminal agent in Europe, could not overthrow him. So once again he changed his tack. But this time he made sure. He chose the most dangerous trade of all—murder!'

'You mean to tell me this beast kills merely to keep himself amused?' I exclaimed in horror. 'That he murders and mutilates to stave off *ennui*?'

'Partly, yes! Certainly in undertaking these hideous crimes his first thought. I believe, has been to bring into being a set of circumstances he cannot stabilise; a situation of ever-increasing personal danger. Formerly he ran no risks. He might as well have been director of a limited company. Whatever came to pass, Moriarty was untouchable. But these killings are another matter. Public opinion is galvanised, and each time the killer ventures out his path is fraught with greater peril. But there is more to it than that. For one thing, Moriarty has clearly determined to make these murders the occasion for a duel to the death with me.'

'With you!'

'Yes, Watson, I am his intended opponent. Of that there can be no doubt. The man wishes to test his mettle. Lestrade and his bobbies are clearly incapable of that. A man like Moriarty might murder the entire female population of London for all the police could do about it. But I have crossed his path, Watson! I have incommoded him. He has felt my check. A lesser man might have been warned off, but not Professor Moriarty. He has thrown down the gauntlet, and from now on we meet face to face. It is an encounter from which only one of us will come away alive.'

'Then these women he kills—'

'Pah! They mean no more to him than counters on a board. He uses them as he uses everyone with whom he comes in contact. Previously it was live thugs; now it is dead drabs. Moriarty sees no difference. He is concerned only with furthering his dread design.'

'His design?'

Holmes nodded grimly.

'I said there is more to these killings than a mere desire for stimulation. To overmaster me is part of his plans, but I fear they go further still. What he intends is nothing less than the overthrow of civilisation as we know it.'

'The man must be mad!'

'If only he were. But he is as sane as myself, and as capable.'

I shook my head emphatically.

'That I cannot believe, Holmes. I saw what he did to that woman in Aldgate. No sane man could have wielded that knife. And then you say he dreams of overthrowing civilisation. Why, what is that but the raving of a maniac!'

Holmes greeted my outburst with quiet laughter.

'If only Moriarty could hear you! You would make him very happy, for you think exactly what he wishes people to think. How brilliantly he has contrived to make all the world believe that he is insane! With what consummate artistry he prompts the *vox populi*! No one knows better than he the emotional value of gore and garters. It is a combination the British find absolutely irresistible.'

'But to disembowel a woman's body—'

'Bleat, my dear Watson! Bleat unmitigated and absolute! How many times have you worked at the dissecting-table, your arms bathed in blood and—'

'Come, Holmes! That's an utterly different case.'

'But why, pray? His corpses were just as dead as yours. Is it only sane to mutilate them inside the walls of a hospital?'

'This is mere sophistry, Holmes!' I exclaimed. 'When a doctor performs a dissection he does so for an excellent reason, which is to enlarge human knowledge. But this monster has no reason for what he does beyond his own twisted desires. That is what makes him insane.'

'And you accuse me of sophistry! My dear Watson, I fear the pot is calling the kettle black. Your argument, like Giotto's O, is remarkable for the perfection of its circularity. You deny that our man has any serious purpose, since his deeds are those of a maniac. When I enquire what is maniacal about them, you reply that it is their lack of purpose. You have demonstrated nothing but the tenacity of your received ideas—as to which, quite frankly, I was never in any real doubt.'

'Then what is his purpose?'

'To create chaos. To work evil.'

'But he was doing far more harm formerly!' I cried. 'You say he controlled the underworld single-handed. What more could he want? What worse can he do?'

'He can destroy the very fabric of civilisation itself,' replied Holmes gravely. 'Formerly he was as much a pillar of society as any captain of industry or financial magnate. No one has a greater vested interest in preserving the *status quo* than your average criminal, for his livelihood depends upon it. When Moriarty was their general, he had no more interest in fomenting anarchy than Mr Gladstone. Certainly his agents robbed and blackmailed and intimidated; even murdered on occasion—but to what end? A few individuals suffered and Moriarty became rich. To a man of the Professor's abstract turn of mind it must have been very clear that, for all his genius, he was merely a petty crook writ large. His desire now is not to magnify mediocrity, but to make himself the instrument of evil itself. Evil cannot be fettered with motive and meaning! It simply strikes at will, and a woman lies gutted on the pavements of London Town. Already he has created a reign of terror unparalleled in this century. Unless I stop him, the cancer he has implanted in Whitechapel will spread and grow until folk are afraid to step out after nightfall, and sit huddled around the fire, starting at a sound. I tell you, Watson, this man means to bring back the Dark Ages! What makes it possible for millions of people to live together in a city such as London? Trust! Destroy trust and you make modern life impossible, and turn our great open city into a camp of armed strangers.'

He paused, staring down at the ground. When he looked up, his eyes burned with a fierce determination.

'Well, he has challenged me. I accept the challenge.'

He broke off suddenly. His gaze was fixed on the path by which we had entered the park. I could see nothing of interest—only an old tramp who was searching the edge of the lake for scraps of bread left by the fowl.

'Come, Watson, it's getting chilly.' Holmes's voice had changed from its discursive tone to one of high urgency. 'I am going away for a few days,' he announced, as we crossed the bridge over the water. 'If anyone asks for me, tell them I am out of the country. As for you, old fellow, take care of yourself. We are engaged with a man who has already murdered five women with cold-blooded venom. It behooves us to be on our guard at all times.'

I was not taken in by this. Whatever the dangers, they threatened no one as much as Holmes himself, and I was determined that he should not face them alone. I therefore offered to accompany him. He refused politely. I insisted. The greater the risks he had to run, the more reason for me to share them with him.

'You have often been glad of my support in the past, Holmes. If this man is the evil genius you claim, it would be mere folly to venture against him alone.'

'You mean well, I know, Watson, but this affair calls not for bulldog tenacity but for quick wits and nimble limbs. You have neither. Now would you kindly summon that four-wheeler and have him stop just by this gate.'

I was deeply hurt by my friend's words. That he could speak to me in such a way was eloquent proof of the terrible strain under which he was labouring. In my heart I forgave him, but I did his bidding coldly and in silence. As the cab drew up, Holmes handed me a scrap of paper on which he had scribbled an address.

'Pass this to the driver, will you? And tell him to make haste.'

I passed this injunction and the note to the cabbie, and then followed Holmes inside. To my amazement, I found the vehicle quite empty. I looked back from the window as we drove away, but the street was deserted, except for the old tramp loitering by the gates. A moment's reflection persuaded me that Holmes must have entered the cab by one door and alighted immediately by the other, thus using the vehicle as cover behind which to slip away down a side-street. I could only hope that this ruse had been successful.

The address to which the cabbie had been directed proved to be 221 Baker Street, and it was there that I spent the following four days—alone, without occupation, and increasingly preoccupied with gloomy forebodings. I knew not what Holmes was doing, nor where he was staying, and since I had no news it was inevitable that I should come to fear the worst. Every morning I opened the paper with trepidation, and though I found nothing to confirm my fears, I could not quiet them. Certainly Holmes was quite capable of defending himself, given a sporting chance, but Moriarty did not sound the type of man who would trouble himself much about the methods he employed.

Finally, as the days dragged slowly by, I made up my mind that if Holmes had still not reappeared by the end of the week, I would call Lestrade and lay the facts before him. Thus when Lestrade himself called at Baker Street on the Thursday morning, my only thought was that he brought word of some dreadful tragedy which had befallen Holmes. His mien was strangely serious, as befits the bearer of evil tidings. I rushed to meet him at the head of the stairs.

'What is it?' I cried wildly. 'Come, let me know the worst!'

Taken unawares, Lestrade stumbled backwards. I took hold of his sleeve as he clutched for the banister. 'Tell me all! What has happened? I must know!'

The official recovered his balance with an effort.

'You didn't ought to do that, Dr Watson,' said he slowly. 'If I had slipped and broke my neck down there, you would have been in serious trouble. Especially when they found this in my pocket.'

He passed me a scruffy envelope. It was addressed to himself, in care of Scotland Yard. There was something oddly familiar about the handwriting. Inside was a letter, scrawled on the cheapest paper. It ran:

Dear Boss,

   I guess you must be having fits never knowing where Ill pop up next   why don't you see a good doctor?

Yours for ever
Jack in the box

No sooner had I read the signature than I knew where I had seen the writing before. It was identical to that of the letter and postcard signed by the murderer of Eddowes and Stride! I looked up at Lestrade.

'It is another letter from the killer.'

The detective nodded.

'And you have come to consult Holmes,' I continued, feeling rather ridiculous after my histrionics. 'Of course! But I fear I must disappoint you. He is not here.'

'No, Doctor, I didn't come to see Mr Holmes. I came to see you.'

'To see me? But why?'

Lestrade produced a small card from his wallet.

'This was enclosed with the letter you have just read.'

I took the card from him, and gasped. I could not have been more surprised if the thing had turned to a pigeon in my hand. Badly stained with blood, but still legible, it was one of my own calling cards!

Lestrade was staring at me expressionlessly.

'But— It's one of my cards!' I spluttered.

'Yes, sir. We were able to spot that, even without Mr Holmes's assistance. The point that interests me is how one of your cards, with blood all over it, came to be included with a letter written—as you yourself admitted—by the Whitechapel killer.'

I stared at the policeman in speechless confusion. I had not seen one of those cards for almost two years. I had had them printed before my association with Holmes had made an independent social life both impossible and unnecessary. Fortunately, I was rescued from my embarrassment by the arrival of a constable bearing a message for the detective. Lestrade read it through, then glanced quickly at the man.

'Wait here,' he ordered him. Then, turning to me, 'Would you have any objection to my taking a look in Mr Holmes's room, Doctor?'

'In Holmes's room? Whatever for?'

He passed me the message he had just received. I read:

You will find what you need on the mantel in Holmes's room. Do not let Dr Watson leave the premises. Retain the constable.

> Abberline*

'Of course, I cannot force you to show me the room without a warrant,' Lestrade continued blandly, 'but I'm sure you can have no objection, as a law-abiding citizen, to my having a look.'

I felt as though I were trapped in some senseless dream from which there was no awakening. But my voice mumbled assent, and we crossed over and passed through the doorway into Holmes's room. Lestrade looked around at the pictures of famous criminals which covered every wall. Then he strode over to the fireplace. The mantelpiece was littered with an assortment of revolver cartridges, knives, pipe dottles, postage stamps, odd coins and so on. But one object stood out boldly from all the rest. It was a medical flask, and it was filled to the brim with a dark red fluid. Lestrade gave a low whistle.

'Blood!' he cried.

'Blood?' I echoed.

'Port,' said a voice from the doorway. We whirled around, to find ourselves under the amused scrutiny of Sherlock Holmes. 'Don't be misled by the container,' he went on. 'It's a Quinta Noval, the '53, and should be quite drinkable. I decanted it myself just the other day.

---

*Inspector Abberline was in charge of the detectives investigating the Whitechapel murders, and would thus have been Lestrade's immediate superior at this time.

But don't take my word for it! There are glasses in the front room, and a fire. Shall we?'

To a disinterested observer, Lestrade and I must have presented a comical spectacle as we filed sheepishly out of Holmes's room. But there was no such observer, as Lestrade at once remarked.

'My constable! Where is he?'

Holmes picked up a coat, a wig, and a beard from the sofa.

'Here he is!'

'You!'

Holmes bowed.

'Then the note you brought was—'

'Counterfeit.'

'And the letter, in the killer's hand?'

'Ditto.'

'But the writing—'

'Phooh! A poor imitation. The "p"s alone should have alerted you.'

'And my card?' I put in.

'Purloined.'

'But the blood?'

'Bovine. Best quality calf's kidney, obtainable at any good butcher's.'

He handed us each a glass of port. Lestrade threw his back as though it were medicine.

'So this is what you call helping the police, is it? Sending us running off on a wild goose chase when we are stretched to breaking point trying to catch a homicidal maniac. I would have thought you would be ashamed to waste our time with this kind of childish practical joking! Mind you, I don't deny that your fancy-dress was very well done. You should have gone on the stage, Mr Holmes. I've said it before—'

'And you will say it again,' interrupted Holmes, unhurriedly filling a pipe.

'No doubt, sir! No doubt. But the theatre is one thing, and real life is another. If you were in a vaudeville I'd be calling for an encore. As it is, I have a good mind to arrest you for impersonating a police officer.'

'But I wouldn't dream of trying to impersonate a police officer, Lestrade! I leave that to you. No, I simply wished to fetch you here, and this seemed as good a way as any. Besides, my little charade was in keeping with the whole tenor of this affair. Has it never struck you that there is a distinctly theatrical thread running right through this Whitechapel case? No? Well, no matter. Away with the theatre! Let us hear from the proponent of real life. What progress have you been making since we last met?'

Lestrade pulled out a cheap cigar and set it alight.

'We are proceeding along various paths of enquiry too numerous to mention. I myself have been making progress in several directions at once, but although we have made great strides, we are not as yet in a position to take any definite steps—'

'Cut it out, Lestrade. Are you any closer to catching this murderer than you were at the same time last month?'

'It's not as simple as you seem to think, Mr Holmes. Rome wasn't—'

'Have you made any progress in a month, Lestrade? Yes or no?'

'We have managed to rule out some of the—'

'Yes or no?'

Lestrade sucked hard at his cigar.

'No. But we are hopeful that—'

'Of course, Lestrade, of course. Hope springs eternal. But I fear that the patience of the British public, although great, is not infinite. Another pair of killings like the last and I imagine you may well be invited to consider the possibilities of a career with the North West Mounted Police.'*

The detective greeted this remark with a rueful expression which suggested that the idea was not altogether new to him.

'There has been a certain amount of criticism, I can-

*The North West Mounted Police became the more familiar Royal Canadian Mounted Police in 1904.

not deny that. Every person in the land, from the hum-
blest of Her Majesty's subjects up to and including Herself, seems to feel they could do a better job of it than
us. The fact is, Mr Holmes, we are being made the
whipping-boys for this country's sins. They've let
Sodom and Gomorrah flourish here in England's green
and pleasant land, and they've looked the other way.
Now this happens, and they take it out on us!'

'Aha!' cried Holmes. 'I always thought I could detect
traces of a Nonconformist upbringing in your character,
Lestrade. But you must be careful, you know! Persons
who go around muttering about Whitechapel being as
the cities of the plain, and its inhabitants the accursed
of the Lord, are very likely, these days, to find themselves the object of suspicion. What was it he said? "I
am down on whores, and I shan't quit ripping them till I
do get buckled." '

Lestrade exhaled a cloud of rancid smoke.

'I'm not down on whores, Mr Holmes. They're a
commodity like any other. But there's no doubt that this
killer can only work as he does because such commerce—and worse—is a fact of life in Whitechapel.
That whole district is a criminal's paradise! No one
knows anything, no one cares to know anything, and no
one would tell us if they did. It's a point of honour with
them to score off the police. Their idea of sport is to get
drunk and knock down a constable. So how are we supposed to go to work? Quite frankly, I believe there's
only one way we'll ever take this man, and that's if
we're lucky enough to come on him while he's actually
killing one of them.'

These last words were spoken defiantly, Lestrade
clearly expecting a sarcastic rejoinder. It was evidently
much to his surprise that he found his old antagonist
agreeing with him.

'That is the first sensible thing I have heard any policeman say since these murders started. After all this
eye-wash about following up leads and investigating
clues and rounding up suspects and developing theories,
it is really very refreshing to hear someone adopting a

realistic attitude at long last. As you say, there is only one way to catch this man, and that's red-handed. More port?'

'With a dash of soda this time, if you please. I'm glad to see we are in agreement for once, Mr Holmes. It is too bad we can do nothing about it. Who's to say when or where he will strike next?'

Holmes hovered by the side-board. He poured port for himself and me, and mixed Lestrade a whisky and soda.

'I am,' he replied as he brought the drinks.

Lestrade laughed politely. 'Come now! We all admit that you are a very smart man, Mr Holmes, and can sometimes spot things that others are too busy to remark. But here you go too far! How can you possibly know what this maniac will do next?'

'Ah, the old sweet song!' murmured Holmes. 'From far and wide they come to behold what the Ripper hath wrought, and cry with one accord: "The work of a maniac!" However, let us suppose that you are right, and that this affair is all madness. If it is, there is still some considerable method in it.'

'Ha! We all know about his methods!'

'Now if we are to take the murderer in the act, we must first know where and when he will be at work. Let us look at his record thus far. All the murders have been committed within the territory bounded by Bishopsgate to the west, the Great Eastern railway to the north, Sidney Street in the east, and the Ratcliff Highway to the south. So much is obvious. Turning to the question of timing, it is also obvious that all the killings have taken place in the morning, between midnight and six o'clock to be precise. What may be less obvious is that there is a clear pattern linking the days on which a murder occurred.'

'What?'

'The first death was on the 7th of August,' Holmes continued evenly. 'On the 31st of the same month Nicholls was killed. Chapman died on the 8th of September, four weeks after Tabram and one week after Nicholls. Thus at that time the sequence ran: a murder, then three weeks' lull, then another murder. But Stride and Eddowes were killed on the last day of September, which is to say three weeks after Chapman. With that the sequence repeats itself, enabling us to identify it as a simple alternation of one and three week periods, with a murder at the end of each.'

Lestrade had pulled out a pocket calendar, over which he bent in concentration. At length he looked up with a triumphant expression.

'Ha! Your sequence no sooner gets started than it breaks down! It appears to have escaped you, Mr Sherlock Holmes, that there was no murder the week following the double killing! How does that fit in with your fine theory?'

Holmes smiled like a conjuror whose bluff has elicited the correct response from the crowd.

'It fits perfectly, my dear Lestrade. You have no doubt heard of the exception that proves the rule? I admit that the absence of any attack on the 7th of October at first surprised me. But instead of rejecting the pattern which had begun to evolve, I reminded myself of a basic principle of our trade—that any single fact which apparently confutes a long chain of reasoning will invariably prove capable of some other interpretation. The lack of any murder that week was no accident but a necessary consequence of the pattern itself. Indeed, it would have been inexplicable if a killing *had* occurred.'

Lestrade shook his head wearily.

'This is all Greek to me.'

'Is it? Let's see if I can't provide you with a crib. The question is what happened to the victim of the 7th October. The answer is simply that she had already been murdered, on the 30th of September.'

'The double murder!' I exclaimed.

'Precisely! Two for the price of one. But Jack the Ripper is not a man to leave his books unbalanced. So to make up for his over-indulgence that bloody Sunday, he abstained the following week. Now then! Do you still think he is a maniac whose deeds are mere random impulses?'

Lestrade wore the expression of one whose world is being taken apart piece by piece and reassembled upside down. He made counting gestures on his fingers. He gazed up at the ceiling. His lips moved soundlessly. At length he looked over at Holmes with a deep sigh.

'So you are saying that this man, whoever he is, has taken it into his head to kill two prostitutes a month, the first after one week and the second three weeks later. Is that it?'

'Not to kill, Lestrade. To mutilate! That is his desire. Killing the women is a mere preliminary, as one kills a goose for the table. If he were satisfied with killing, he would have gone straight home after cutting Stride's throat. Instead, he exposed himself to enormous danger so that he might suitably butcher the woman in Mitre Square. Do you remember that message he left scrawled on the wall in Goulston Street—the one your ineffable superiors had erased before it could be photographed?'

' "The Jews are not the men that will be blamed for nothing," ' I quoted from memory. Holmes nodded.

'There have been any number of attempts to explain those words,' he went on. 'The spelling of Jews— J,U,W,E,S,—has been analysed as learnedly as if it were an Egyptian hieroglyph, though one might have thought that this man had already given us sufficient evidence of his penchant for eccentric spellings. But what no one has been able to demonstrate is who the Jews in question are, and what it is they are to be blamed for.'

'And I suppose you find it all very simple,' Lestrade muttered.

Holmes shrugged nonchalantly. 'The truth is invariably simple. The problem is clearing away the undergrowth of falsehood. The Jews referred to are the inhabitants of that courtyard in Berner Street, and more particularly Louis Diemschutz, the hawker whose untimely return home prevented the killer from mutilating Stride's body. What they are to be blamed for is the heinous crime of upsetting our man's timetable, so that he was forced to move his next killing forward a week. He was saying, in effect: "I apologise for the confusion, but it wasn't my fault—those Jews are to blame." '

Lestrade was by now swaying in his seat, like some punch-drunk boxer.

'But how could he know the fellow was a Jew?' He croaked. 'How could he possibly know?'

'Because the courtyard is occupied by a notorious Socialists' Club run by and for European Jews. It is a hundred to one that anyone coming or going there at that time of night will be Jewish. Which all goes to prove, if any further proof were needed, how well our man knows his Whitechapel.'

At this, Lestrade's resistance utterly collapsed. He looked helplessly at my friend.

'What do we do?'

Holmes sprang to his feet.

'We patrol! We shut up Whitechapel like a cage! According to the sequence, the next killing is due within a few days. But we can determine the timing even more closely than that. For one thing, the murders always take place at the weekend—with the exception of Tabram, which I am inclined to see as something of a prentice job. To be even more specific, the death days—again leaving Tabram out of account—have been Friday, Saturday, and Sunday respectively. All of which suggests that the attempt will be made on Monday. In any event, only four nights are involved, and only four hours a night. If we cannot adequately patrol an area of one square mile for that period of time, I think we had better retire and have done with it.'

Lestrade was now on familiar ground again, and he nodded with more assurance.

'It can be done.'

'It must be done, and done consummately! I shall call at the Yard this afternoon at five with details of such measures as I consider necessary. In the meantime you must summon every available man on the force and have them ready to commence duty at midnight.'

The official scratched his ear uneasily.

'I'll certainly do whatever I can, Mr Holmes. I am quite happy to accept your lead myself, you understand, but my superiors—'

'Will back you all the way. You may be interested to learn that I now enjoy the rank of Acting Chief Inspector in your own division. As you said, criticism of the way the police have been handling this affair extends to the highest quarters. My brother Mycroft informed me last week that it was the wish of one more accustomed to command that I should exert my energies in this regard. It has been my pleasure as well as my duty to obey. I made it a condition, however, that I might implement just such measures as I have mentioned. The appropriate arrangements have been made, and you need therefore have no qualms about carrying out my instructions.'

'Very good, Mr Holmes. I quite understand. I'll expect you about five, sir. Good day.'

Never had I seen Lestrade so amenable. Holmes had also remarked the change in the policeman's manner.

'By Jove, Watson!' said he, once we were alone again. 'If this ghastly business has achieved nothing else, it seems at least to have taught the Yard its natural limits. However, I have no very lively hopes that the effect will last. And now would you be so good as to summon our landlady? I am in urgent need of a bath, some hot food, and a few hours' undisturbed sleep. I have been deprived of all three just lately. In fact it has been quite an eventful week, what with one thing and another. One of my little "Holmes from home" was set alight in the early hours of yesterday morning. No great damage was done, but I lost my night's sleep in consequence.'

'Good God! You mean the fire was deliberately started?'

'I think we may assume so, in view of the three other attempts that have been made on my life recently. Any other hypothesis would seem to introduce a monstrous factor of sheer coincidence. Professor Moriarty is not a man to let grass grow under his feet! He first attempted to run me down with a delivery van. My reactions were too quick, but shortly thereafter a brick fell from a building as I was passing and almost scrambled my brains. His latest effort was delegated. I was walking down a secluded street in Islington late last night, when a pair of ruffians assaulted me with cudgels.'

'What did I tell you? You should have kept me at your side! You might have been killed!'

'Oh, they weren't very competent ruffians. I exercised some of my singlestick skills on them. One fled and the other succumbed. I barked my knuckles, as you see, but I'm otherwise none the worse.'

'But next time he will send more men, and better! You must have protection, Holmes! You must not go out alone! I absolutely forbid it!'

Holmes smiled at my vehemence.

'My dear fellow! In a moment you will be saying: "As your physician—" But you need not distress yourself. Moriarty does not mean to kill me yet.'

'But you told me—'

'I told you that there have been attempts on my life. Attempts, Watson! If Moriarty wanted me killed, I should be reposing in some gutter by now. No, he only means to keep me on my guard. He is playing for his life after all. It would hardly be fair if I did not stand to lose as much.'

I shook my head in disapproval.

'I do not see how you can speak of playing fair with this kind of man. Why do you allow him his sport? Why do you delay? Why not tell Lestrade and have him arrested? Then we shall all be safe—you, me, and all these poor women.'

'I understand your feelings, Watson. I have felt the same. But it cannot be. How can we arrest Moriarty? What grounds have we? On the basis of what evidence are we to charge him? My suspicions are at bottom all inference and supposition, and if I were to mention them to Lestrade he would laugh in my face. But Moriarty would not laugh! He would summon his legal advisers and obtain his unconditional release, and then his revenge would be dreadful to behold. No, let us be grateful that we know the devil with whom we have to deal, and that he is content to fight this duel with me. Let us observe the rules of honour, and press our advantage home. Believe me, Watson—therein lies our only hope of smashing this man's tyranny.'

I was reluctantly compelled to admit the force of Holmes's arguments. But before he retired I had wrung from him a promise that I might accompany him at all times throughout the perilous hours that lay ahead. No longer would I be content to sit patiently at home awaiting the outcome. When Holmes left for Scotland Yard that afternoon, I went with him, a revolver in my pocket and in my heart the determination to stick close to his side wherever he might go and whatever might befall. I have often wondered to what extent the holocaust that was to come was due precisely to my success in this endeavour.

# Three

A close account of the next four nights would offer only needless drudgery for writer and reader alike. Indeed, without considerable invention on my part it would not even be possible. I was too tired and dispirited to keep my notes, and my memory retains nothing beyond a general sense of weary futility. Our good fortune was restricted to the weather, which was unseasonably mild. As Lestrade sarcastically remarked, if one had to search Whitechapel by night for someone who wasn't there one couldn't wish for better weather, considering the time of year.

Holmes's plan had been to swamp the entire area with police. He had calculated that the murderer would require at least ten minutes to kill and mutilate his victim, and he had accordingly drawn up a system of patrols which left no street unvisited for longer than that. The net was duly fashioned and thrown over Whitechapel. The three of us established ourselves at the Commercial Street police station and awaited developments. There were none. Holmes and I made outings from time to time to ensure that the patrols were observing the specified timetable. Occasionally a man would be a minute or two out, but we found no significant gaps in the mesh. There was simply nothing to be caught. By six o'clock on Monday morning it was clear that all our efforts had been in vain. The patrols were disbanded and we three assembled before a waning fire at the police station, grasping mugs of lukewarm tea. Lestrade was the only one to display any animation, and this was of a malicious cast. As the nights had gone by without incident the little official's habitual swank and swagger had gradually replaced the awed subservience to which he had been reduced by the brilliance of Holmes's arguments that Thursday in Baker Street. Thus far he had said nothing, no doubt fearing that his hated rival might yet be proved right at the last. But now Holmes's time was up, and Lestrade turned the tables with vindictive relish.

'What do you say now, Mr Sherlock Holmes? What has become of your blessed sequence with everything worked out to the last detail, as if it was the tides we were waiting for and not a homicidal maniac? Admit it, you have failed!'

Holmes's reply was barely audible.

'On the contrary, Inspector, I have succeeded all too well.'

'Oh ho, I see! That's the way we play, is it? Heads you win and tails we lose! I only wish my job was that easy. But it's not you will have to take the blame for this fiasco. You who are always so careful to keep your name out of the press! Very wise, I'm sure! A fine time of it I'm in for, trying to explain why every spare man on the force has been pounding the beat in Whitechapel these four nights. Mind you, there was only one thing wrong with your timetable, Mr Holmes. No one told the murderer about it! Ha ha! That's where you went wrong! You told us when the next murder was due, but you forgot to tell him! You should have told him too, Mr Holmes, and then he might have obliged us after all!'

To my surprise, Holmes did not rise to these barbs. He listened in silence, his head bowed. It was an odd attitude for one who normally impressed all and sundry with his masterful manner. But clearly the setback he had received had shaken him severely. Lestrade was not deterred by the lack of any response. Long and bitter were the tirades he unleashed. He recalled Holmes's overweening confidence, his arrogant refusal to consider the proposals of others, his contempt for the traditional techniques of investigation long proved effective—in practice, mind you, not in some smoky sitting-room!—by the appointed guardians of law and order of whom he had the honour and, yes, the pleasure to be one. When he finally recognised that my friend was not going to be drawn, Lestrade revealed his ace. He took a file from his desk and withdrew a sheet of paper which he handed to us in turn. It was the original of a letter which had been published some weeks earlier in the press. It ran as follows:

From hell

Mr Lusk
   Sor

      I send you half the kidne I took from one woman presarved it for you tother piece I fried and

ate it was very nise I may send you the bloody knif
that took it out if you only wate a whil longer.
                    Signed                    Catch me when
                                                    you can
                                        Mishter Lusk


I must add that this transcription cannot possibly do
justice to the impression produced by the original. The
letter was written in a crabbed and violent hand, and
was exceedingly difficult to make out. It was the most
utterly malevolent-looking piece of writing I have ever
set eyes on. Holmes glanced at it perfunctorily, and then
handed it back to Lestrade without comment. The official held it up before our eyes.

'You remember the other two letters we received, the
ones signed "Jack the Ripper"?' said he. 'They were
genuine enough, for the writer knew more than he
should about those murders. However, this letter here is
genuine too!'

'How can you tell?' I demanded, since Holmes remained silent.

'Good question, Dr Watson! I'm glad you asked.
How can we tell? Enclosed with this letter was part of a
human kidney, just like it says. Mr Lusk, who heads the
vigilantes, sent it to the City Police, and they sent it on
to the London Hospital. There it was looked at by the
pathologist, who declares there is no doubt that it came
from the murdered woman Eddowes. The letter must
therefore be from her murderer. But as you can see for
yourselves, the writing is totally different from all the
other specimens, including that on the wall in Goulston
Street.'

He paused significantly. Holmes yawned and consulted his watch. 'And what conclusion do you draw
from that?' he murmured.

'Why, surely a smart man like yourself doesn't need
to ask me that!' cried the detective with a great show of
surprise. 'The conclusion is quite obvious, as far as I
can see.'

'No doubt, Inspector, but I have never been able to

determine just how far that is. At all events, what do
you conclude from the difference in the hands?'

'But it can mean only one thing! There must be two
murderers!'

The slight figure in the raffish check suit visibly
preened with triumph. His eyes glinted with pride. I noticed, not for the first time, how remarkably close-set
they were.

Holmes got to his feet. He fetched his coat and put it
on. 'Well, I think we should be going. Are you ready,
Watson? Many thanks for your hospitality, Inspector.
You will doubtless present us in due course with an opportunity of returning it.'

Lestrade could scarcely control his fury. He danced
from one foot to the other, waving the letter at Holmes.

'Is that your reply? Is that all you have to say? Well
that's what I call grateful! Your fancy theory goes all to
smash, and when I offer you a helping hand you haven't
a word to say!'

'As a matter of fact I have several, but I very much
doubt whether you would wish to hear them. Good
morning, Inspector. Come, Watson!'

We walked briskly to Shoreditch High Street, where
we found a cab to take us home. Not one word would
Holmes say, and I was too exhausted to make conversation. As soon as we arrived at 221B, Holmes disappeared into his room, locking the door after him. For
my part, I stretched out on the sofa and leafed through
the papers. Within a few minutes I dozed off, and slept
until I was awakened by the maid come to dust.

At lunch I was both surprised and delighted to find
that Holmes was once more his usual urbane self. He
dispatched Billy to Dolamore's for a bottle of hock, and
while we ate and drank he held forth on a number of
subjects ranging from the art of the troubadours to the
possibility of using electricity as a means of capital punishment. He did not mention the subject that was, however, uppermost in both our minds. When we were both
settled before the fire with our cigars, I decided that the
time had come to grasp the nettle.

'I say, Holmes, what did happen? What went wrong?'

For a moment I thought I had blundered. My friend looked up at me with hurt in his eyes, and an expression that seemed to say '*Et tu, Brute?*' But the next instant he laughed, though it was perhaps rather forced.

'Are you a Brother of the Angle, Watson?'

'I beg your pardon?'

'Have you fished?'

'Upon occasion.'

'Then you will be aware that the critical juncture occurs just when your game is nibbling at the bait. Pull too fast and the hook will miss him; too slow, and he will be off with his supper, leaving you with none. These four nights past we have been angling for Moriarty. The unfortunates of Whitechapel were our bait and my patrols the hook. But I was too eager. Not that our work was by any means wasted, for we certainly prevented another murder. But I had set my sights on taking the Professor at his work, and there I failed.'

I regarded Holmes steadily through a haze of cigar smoke.

'Moriarty was there, then?'

'Certainly he was there. He studied the network of police patrols I had instituted, noted that it was flawless, and retired, gnashing his teeth.'

'Then you did not fail! We have beaten him!'

Holmes shook his head slowly.

'No, Watson. On the contrary, we may have lost everything. If he were to change his method or his sequence, we should be all at sea once again. Ah, but Watson, imagine his rage! Think what frustration and resentment must be his! He challenged me to a duel, and I have forestalled him. There can be little question that he will now step up his attempts to eliminate me. And therein lies our salvation.'

'Holmes! What are you saying!'

'That we must keep him to his sequence at all costs! His next attempt is not due until the weekend after next. Somehow or other we must occupy his attention until then. Now if I can lure him out of London and keep him entertained until Thursday week, I believe there is an excellent chance that we may still come out of this affair with credit.'

I was horrified by this proposal, and protested long and volubly, but to no effect. Holmes argued that his life was at risk in any case, and that it was actually to his advantage to leave town.

'Moriarty knows and uses this city as if it were a machine he had personally designed. In the country we shall be on a more equal footing. I rather fancy Wiltshire would suit. It has always attracted me from the train; here is a splendid opportunity to know it better.'

Seeing that any attempt to dissuade him was doomed to end in failure, I demanded the right to accompany him and to share whatever hardships and dangers lay in store. But once again he refused, and when I insisted he permitted himself some unkind comments on my physical capabilities. At this I fell silent. As soon as I ceased to argue, Holmes applied the balm.

'Don't look so cast down, old fellow. Your role may appear less glamorous than you could wish, but it is a vital one. It is up to you to hold the fort here, and to keep my base secure. And in the event of my failing to return—'

'Holmes!'

'If I fail to return, I say, by nine o'clock in the evening of the 8th, then you must summon Lestrade and hand him the envelope of papers which you will find in pigeon-hole M. I am afraid that it will be like setting Newton's calculus before an Esquimau, but I will naturally do what I can to ensure that the situation does not arise. No, not another word! I am going out now to attend to some business. After dinner I expect to feel a craving for bright lights and milling throngs. A visit to the music hall would, I fancy, supply both. May I count on your company? It is always salutary to remind oneself that for every man who thrills to Patti's "Una voce poco fa" there are ten who would sooner listen to Bessie Bellwood's rendition of "What cheer 'Ria".'

I was agreeably surprised by Holmes's suggestion.

After some of the so-called entertainments to which I had accompanied him, it was indeed pleasant to be able to contemplate an evening of real enjoyment. We went to the Oxford,* and I for one had a grand time. I completely forgot all our recent tribulations in the many and varied attractions of the skilfully arranged programme. As act followed act I willingly surrendered to the spell of each artiste—laughing with this one, weeping with that, and joining in the chorus of songs both patriotic and sentimental. I could not remember having enjoyed myself more; but all good things must end, and when the show was over my pleasure was distinctly marred by the discovery that Holmes had disappeared. I searched high and low, I questioned the attendants, I waited for fifteen minutes outside, but at last I was forced to concede that my companion had simply deserted me in mid-evening without so much as troubling to take his leave. I walked back to Baker Street in some considerable disgruntlement. But once I had given the matter some thought I ceased to be quite as surprised, though I remained extremely annoyed at his shabby behaviour. No doubt Holmes had found the proceedings at the Oxford dreadfully common. His taste, as I knew to my cost, inclined more towards highfalutin foreign fairy tales that go on and on for five hours without one hummable tune. There was indeed a distinctly snobbish strain in my friend's blood, which caused him to shun the pleasures of the people on principle. It was one of the trifling peccadilloes which reminded one that he was, after all, only human.

There was no sign of Holmes at 221B, however, and when he had still not returned the next morning I began to wonder if I had been mistaken. Was the explanation of this mystery perhaps more sinister than I had realised? Then, just before lunch, a telegram arrived. It had been handed in at Devizes and read: 'Hare off and run-

---

*Long demolished, the Oxford Theatre went through four different incarnations at 26–32 Oxford Street. Holmes and Watson will have visited the third version, which stood from 1873 until 1892.

ning. Hounds hard at heel. Going moderate to heavy. Holmes.' I looked up from this message, and in my mind's eye I scanned the bleak windswept uplands of Salisbury Plain and the Wiltshire Downs. All at once this plan of Holmes's appeared horribly double-edged. If Moriarty was removed from his haunts and helpers, so too was Holmes himself from the refuges and resources of the city none knew better than he. Out in those ancient unpeopled wildernesses he was utterly alone, and might be hunted down and killed like any solitary animal.

'No news, good news' runs the proverb, but as the days passed with no further word from Holmes, it came to seem a very hollow comfort. Any news, however unwelcome, would at least have banished my unrestrained conjectures. But nine days passed without even a crumb of comfort. Then, on the evening before Holmes was due to return, I made a singular and rather disturbing discovery. It happened in this way. I was sitting before the fire, a book lying unread before me, thinking over the steps I should have to take the following evening if my friend did not reappear. This train of thought led me to recall the envelope of papers which Holmes had instructed me to give Lestrade. Before long I began to speculate on the contents of this packet. What further revelations of Moriarty's character and misdeeds might it not contain? There could be no harm in my looking through papers of such an impersonal nature. I fetched the envelope from its cubicle in Holmes's desk, and tore it open. The contents literally staggered me. The document I was to pass on to the police in the event of Holmes's death, representing all that was known about the Whitechapel murderer, consisted of five sheets of perfectly blank foolscap.

For a minute or two I considered the possibility of invisible inks and suchlike, but I was soon forced to accept that the entire business of the 'all-important papers' and my 'vital mission' had been nothing but a contrivance to silence my protests at being left behind.

Holmes must have known that whatever evidence he had gathered would be useless—indeed perhaps meaningless—to anyone but himself. He had simply staked all on his ability to outwit the Professor and return in person to conclude the case no one else was equipped to prosecute. But what if he had miscalculated? Supposing Moriarty came off best after all? What was I to do if Holmes did not appear by nine o'clock the following evening? What was I to tell Lestrade? I knew virtually nothing definite about Moriarty, for Holmes had been decidedly reticent when it came to details. He had omitted to say which university the Professor had resigned from, for instance, or where he had been living in London. I hardly even knew what he was supposed to look like! Holmes had described him as tall and thin, with deeply sunken eyes and rounded shoulders, pale and ascetic in appearance. It was a striking sketch, but it was hardly a basis for identifying an otherwise unknown man. In short, it was evident that the possibility of failure had never occurred to Holmes, or if it had he had refused to entertain it. All he had gained, and all we stood to lose, he had hazarded on the chance of his returning from Wiltshire in time to forestall Moriarty in the streets of Whitechapel. I could only pray that his confidence might not prove to have been mistaken.

But by dinner hour on Thursday night there was still no sign of my friend. With a heavy heart I ordered Mrs Hudson to send up the roast, of which I partook sparingly. I had no more appetite than a man on the eve of his execution. As the clock struck nine I was toying disconsolately with my pudding when the faintest sound alerted all my senses. I was sitting in my usual place, facing the windows, and the sound I had heard was behind me. Someone was in Holmes's room! I sprang up from my chair and turned to face the intruder. I do not know whom I expected to see there—Moriarty, perhaps, with Holmes's blood on his hands and his eyes full of murder. But the sight that greeted me was very different. Lounging against the jamb, resplendent in evening dress, was the man over whose fate I had been agonising for the past ten days.

'Sorry to startle you, Watson.'

'Holmes! I thought you would never get here!'

'Yes, I fear I have made rather a fetish of punctuality on this occasion. I meant to be with you sooner, but the catch on my window proved unexpectedly intransigent.'

'But won't you eat something? You must be famished.'

'No, thank you. I had a late lunch at the Diogenes Club. But I'll smoke a cigar with you, while we wait for Lestrade.'

'Lestrade! But he has refused to work with you again. He as good as said so last week!'

My friend settled himself before the fire.

'My dear Watson, Inspector Lestrade may fancy himself a free agent, but in practice he is a paid employee and does exactly what his superiors tell him to do. On this occasion he has been ordered to assist me in any way I direct. I sent him his instructions late last night and I expect our good George here in person on the stroke of ten.'

'Last night? But surely then you were—'

'If you insist on the Socratic method,' said Holmes, as he lit his cigar, 'this is going to take an intolerable time. Will you not settle for a simple narrative, with a period for questions at the end?'

I nodded.

'I suppose I should begin by apologising for my abrupt departure from the theatre on Monday night. To be honest, my real motive in going there was to facilitate my departure from London. I should have liked to tell you what I was about, but it would never have done. You cannot dissemble, my dear fellow! It is one of your chief charms. Moriarty would have known at once that something was afoot, and with such a pugilist one cannot afford to telegraph one's punches. He followed us to the Oxford, of course, but I was able to lose him in the crowd, though one of his agents must have spotted me at the door. I left at a quarter to nine, taking a cab to Paddington, where I was just in time to catch the last train to the West of England. Moriarty was not to be put off so easily, however. He immediately commanded a special, which was speedily prepared, the lines being clear at that hour. My train made but four or five stops, and Moriarty observed the same itinerary, enquiring at each station whether a man of my description had alighted there. By this simple process he soon discovered that my destination had been Chippenham. He was barely an hour behind me.

'Chippenham does not offer such a wealth of options to the weary traveller that Moriarty had much trouble in determining at which inn I had put up. But fortunately for myself, and the other inhabitants of that historic pile, the landlord is not used to receiving guests in the small hours. It was only by long and loud resort to the bell that Moriarty gained entrance, and by then both I and my suspicions had been aroused. I dressed hurriedly and left by way of the roof. That incident set the style for all our subsequent encounters. For eight days, Watson, we have played at cat and mouse over Salisbury Plain and the Vale of Pewsey. Imagine if you can a chess game between two masters, such that each must not only plan his every move but execute it too, in person, and on a board the size of an English county. Such is the game with which Moriarty and I have been passing the time since you last saw me. It has proved highly diverting. For instance, if you have been wondering why I chose to climb in through my bedroom window this evening, instead of making a more conventional entrance, the answer is that I wished first to satisfy myself that you were indeed Dr Watson.'

I must have given Holmes a very strange look at this, for he smiled wryly.

'Don't worry, old fellow, the strain of the past week has not unbalanced my mind. But that inn at Chippenham is not the only one I have been obliged to quit at short notice. There was also the occasion of your interesting appearance in the little village of West Lavington.'

'But this is absurd!' I cried. 'I have not been out of London all week!'

'Therein lies the interest. I was awakened at dawn with the news that a Dr Watson was come from London with an urgent communication from Scotland Yard. I was naturally suspicious, and positioned myself so as to have a clear view of the stairway. Down went the boy, and a moment later who should appear but—you! I was surprised and delighted, and my immediate impulse, of course, was to go and greet you. Had I yielded, it is very doubtful whether I should ever have left that picturesque hamlet, save perhaps in a coffin.'

'Good God!'

'It was Moriarty. But he had you to the life, my dear Watson! In fact I should assuredly be gathered to the collective bosom of my forebears by now, had he not made one trivial error.'

'What?'

'Your gammy leg.'

'My leg!'

'Yes, Watson, if you are ever again tempted to curse the *jezail* bullet which shattered your heel, ended your military career, and can seriously incommode you even today—pause and consider that but for that wound Sherlock Holmes would be no more.'

'But I don't see how—'

'You do not need me to remind you that it was your left heel which the bullet struck. The Watson who came to meet me at that village inn limped to perfection, but it was his right leg he favoured. I spotted it just in time, and slammed the door in his face. I then leapt from the window and melted away into the twilight of the Plain. But you will appreciate that after that I have become somewhat sceptical of appearances.'

'By Jove, Holmes! If the fellow had got away with his dastardly plot, I would have been charged with your murder!'

'Precisely. Professor Moriarty is by no means devoid of a certain macabre sense of humour, although it is only to be had at a price most people would consider too dear by half.'

The bell sounded below-stairs, and Holmes leapt to his feet. He rushed over to the door and turned the key in the lock.

'Fetch your revolver, Watson!' he whispered urgently. 'This may well be another of his jests.'

I had barely time to get the weapon out of my desk when someone rapped loudly on the panel of the door.

'Who's there?' cried Holmes, standing well to one side.

'Inspector Lestrade.'

Hearing the familiar nasal voice, I at once relaxed. Holmes, however, made no move to unlock the door.

'Do you recall the St Simon wedding case, Lestrade?'

There was a brief silence before the official answered.

'Mr Holmes, I haven't come all this way to play at—'

'Now, now! Do you recall it or not?'

'Of course I recall it. It was only last month.'

'Then you will remember discovering the bride's clothing in the Serpentine, and informing me that you were dragging for her body.'

'I do, but what the devil—'

'Now listen carefully, for this is very important. Can you recall my reply?'

Once again there was a brief silence. Holmes tensed perceptibly.

'I'm not likely to forget any of your little jibes, Mr Holmes,' the voice returned bleakly. 'I believe you said that I would do as well to drag the basin of the Trafalgar Square fountain.'

My friend at once stepped forward and threw open the door.

'Come in, Lestrade. I must apologise for the challenge, but it was a necessary precaution. We have had a bad case of foes posing as friends just recently.'

'Trouble with imposters, is it?' enquired the policeman, stepping warily into the room. 'It sounds to me as if you need protection, Mr Holmes. I should get in touch with the police if I were you.'

Holmes smiled thinly.

'I fear I am totally incapable of conceiving any circumstances in which you might be me, Inspector. Besides, I have every hope that following our operations tonight the problem will cease to exist.'

Lestrade raised his eyebrows and returned Holmes's smile.

'So you still believe the murderer is going to show up, eh? Regular as the almanac, eh, Mr Holmes?'

'If you were slightly less obtuse you would be able to see it yourself. That latest letter of his explicitly admits what I stated at the time—that he had been on the point of committing another outrage when he was disturbed by our patrols. What were his words? "Just as I was going to draw me knife along her blooming throat them curses of coppers spoilt the game." It is over a month since our man last tasted blood. He will be at work tonight, you may be sure of that. The only question is, will we be ready for him? I take it, Lestrade, that the arrangements you were instructed to make have in fact been seen to?'

'You'll have nothing to complain of on that score. Everything has been done as you directed.'

'Then let us delay no longer. Come, gentlemen! We must not keep Jack the Ripper waiting!'

It was a cold and blustery night, and we pulled our coats close about us as the four-wheeler Lestrade had brought rolled eastwards through the emptying city. The bleak prospect on every side seemed in complete accord with the nature of our business. The only signs of activity, indeed, were the gangs at work sweeping and sanding the streets for the Lord Mayor's procession the following morning. Holmes pointed out these festal preparations.

'There is yet another reason for feeling confident we shall see our man tonight. You must have remarked how he craves publicity. How could he pass over the chance to steal the Lord Mayor's show with a bloodbath in Whitechapel? Every newspaper in the world would put out a special edition for such a story!'

Lestrade grunted contemptuously.

'To hear you talk, anyone would think the killer was a friend of yours. You seem to know his mind better than he does himself.'

' "*Humani nil a me alienum puto*," ' replied Holmes sententiously. 'As long as you continue to believe, along with Tom, Dick, and Harry, that this affair is merely an English translation of *The Murders in the Rue Morgue*, so long are you going to remain in the dark. The secret of my success is simply that while everyone else has been wasting their time searching for a gorilla in human form, I have been looking for a man who for reasons of his own has chosen to assume a gorilla costume.'

'Your success!' cried the Scotland Yarder harshly. 'That's a good one, I'm sure. Another success like your last one will cost me my job! Don't talk to me of your success! I don't want to hear about it, or your gorillas either! I just wish I had a relative in Whitehall to square things with the bigwigs. Then you might see a thing or two, Mr Sherlock Holmes, and never mind your blessed gorillas!'

By the end of this speech the little man was almost incoherent with rage. Holmes regarded him icily.

'I really don't know that that is any way to speak to a superior officer, Lestrade,' said he.

Our drive was completed in silence. We alighted at the same police station in Commercial Street which had been the scene of our vigils a fortnight earlier. The building was once more a hive of activity. A fire was roaring in the grate, and Holmes and I made haste to warm ourselves after the draughty cab ride. Lestrade, however, pointedly took himself off to join his fellow detectives at the other side of the room. This group ignored the two of us from the moment we entered the room, although the resident constabulary were friendly enough and pressed mugs of tea on us. But Lestrade's pique in being forced to co-operate with the hated amateur was obviously shared by his colleagues from the

Yard. Holmes took not the slightest notice of their display of ill-feeling.

'I am here to catch a murderer,' said he, 'not to fraternise with a class of individuals whose conversational resources generally begin and end with the injunction that anything one says may be taken down and used in evidence.'

On one wall of the room was posted a large plan of the district, marked with a great number of different coloured lines representing patrol routes, and circles with various symbols corresponding to the specified timings at given points. All this Holmes explained to me as we studied the system he had drawn up. I was enormously impressed by the thoroughness and skill with which the complicated web had been woven. Truly, nothing seemed to have been left to chance.

'With such defences as these, it must be impossible for the killer to strike with impunity,' I declared.

Holmes looked grave.

'I sincerely hope he does not agree with you.'

'What? But you cannot wish him to succeed?'

'By no means. But it is essential that he should be drawn into making the attempt. The principle underlying this complex of patrols is to allow him to do just that, and to take him in the act. I might add that formulating it has proved the third hardest intellectual exercise of my life. Without Mycroft's assistance I should never have managed it in time. We completed the final details only last night. It made for a very tricky piece of applied mathematics, I can assure you. But then the whole case, really, has been of such exceptional interest. It is almost a pity to think that it may all be history by morning!'

For several minutes I studied the plan in silence. Then I sighed deeply, and smote my palm with my fist.

'How this waiting galls me! If we could only do something!'

'As a matter of fact, we can,' murmured Holmes.

'When a crime is reported, yes! Until then we can

only wait on the murderer's pleasure. He might be anywhere out there.'

I waved at the map on the wall. Holmes took a sheet
of paper and a pencil from the table.

'He might be, yes. But I have an idea I know just
where he is. Look at this.'

He passed me the paper, on which he had drawn this
design:

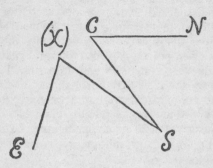

'What do you make of it?' enquired Holmes with a
smile.

'It looks like one of those beastly things we had to
copy at school. Some ancient Greek thought them up as
a punishment for innocent children.'

'I take it you are referring to Euclid's theorems in
plane geometry. The comparison is flattering—indeed
not unapt—but my little sketch has no musty school-
room smell about it. It is simply a diagram showing the
position of Moriarty's last four murders. The letter N
indicates the point where Nicholl's body was found; C
similarly stands for Chapman, S for Stride, and E for
Eddowes.'

'And X, I suppose stands for the unknown—the
next victim. But how can you tell where to place it?'

'Ah! Let me just turn the figure slightly this way,
like so. Now what do you see?'

For a moment I simply stared stupidly at the paper.
Then, all at once, I had it.

'It is a letter M!'

'Exactly, Watson. It is a capital M. M for murder. M for—'

'Moriarty! My God, Holmes, do you mean to tell me—'

'That he is inscribing his initial upon the face of White-chapel in human blood! You may remember that a letter M was found scrawled upon an envelope beside the body of Chapman. His first thought, no doubt, was to leave some such clue at the scene of each murder, like an artist signing a canvas. Then a bigger and better idea occurred to him—an idea which exemplifies to perfection the qualities of twisted humour, bestial genius and absolute egotism of which his character is composed.'

I looked again at the design.

'It's a trifle lopsided, isn't it?'

'Indeed it is, though through no fault of the Professor's. In fact the distortion of his initial sheds yet more light on that message on the wall. For this too, "the Jews" are to blame. The sites of the first three killings were perfectly calculated. There can be no doubt that each crime was coldly premeditated. You will note that the trio forms an equilateral triangle with a side of exactly one kilometre. To complete his design, Moriarty needed to create a second triangle identical to the first and sharing a common apex—the yard in Berner Street where Stride was killed. The result would have been a huge letter M, each stroke being one kilometre in length. The fourth murder was therefore meant to take place in the lower Minories, close by the Blackwall railway line. A fifth killing in the Brushfield Street area would then have completed the figure, as Moriarty would have lost no time in pointing out to the press. However, this ingenious and ambitious undertaking was irreparably damaged when he was forced to extemporise his fourth killing. Mind you, he did not do at all badly, all things considered. Mitre Square is almost exactly one kilometre from Berner Street, but unfortunately it is a little too far north for him to be able to complete his initial as he wished. He will have to settle for an M that is decidedly bent, though still recognisable, and to achieve that he must stage his fifth murder somewhere in the streets not far to the south of this station, by the new market. That is where I expect him to strike, and that is where I shall go to meet him.'

'Not without me!'

'My dear fellow, if you wish to accompany me—'

'I insist upon it.'

'I expected as much. One moment, whilst I invent some suitable tale to tell Lestrade.'

'Tell him the truth.'

'Oh, he would never believe that!'

It was shortly before midnight when Holmes and I emerged from the police station. For the next hour I found myself being led through a warren of lanes and alleys whose existence I had until then only read about. Our previous forays had all been made by carriage, and had been confined to the main thoroughfares. Now for the first time I saw in detail and at close quarters the milieu which Jack the Ripper had chosen for his ghastly sport.

At the time, the popular impression of the murderer was of a great strapping brute swathed in black who skulked through deserted and fog-bound streets until he met up with the one unescorted and attractive female who was also abroad. The passing years have added their seal of authority to this notion, and today no one thinks to question it. As one who was there, I must protest that it is a complete travesty of the actual circumstances, and one that considerably devalues their real horror. What lent these crimes their almost supernatural aura was the fact that they were committed on perfectly clear nights, and in streets that were if anything busier and better lit at that hour than most others in the city. The lighting was largely provided by the lodging-houses. These huge brick barns, containing hundreds of beds to rent by the night, each carried a lamp suspended above its front entrance as a beacon to guide the footsteps of its patrons, who, coming and going as they did at all hours, in turn accounted for the relative busyness of the streets compared with those of more respectable and better ordered districts. Throughout the night this tide of humanity, though it might slacken, continued to run. No sooner did the beer-shops let out than the lodging-houses took in, and at all times there was the constant trickle of those too poor to hire a bed, those in search of the bars that never closed, those too drunk to find their way, those too exhausted to care, those in fractious mood, and those bent on larceny or worse. And finally—as impossible to forget as they were to ignore—there were those women whose labours began when their honest sisters sought their rest, and whose trade was plied in the hours when conscience slumbers and shame hides its face.

I have no family to consider, so there can be no harm now in confessing that I sowed a few wild oats in my youth. Medicine is not a subject one can study from an ivory tower. The facts of life and death pass daily before one's eyes, and the result for the student body is a certain communal moral laxity which, precisely because it is communal, remains essentially innocent. In a word, it was a question of going along with the other fellows or being taken for a nancy-boy. Then, too, we were in London, where anything may be had for a price—and in those days the price was generally not exorbitant. The upshot, at any rate, was that I had seen something of life as it was lived in that warren of streets off the Haymarket. But despite this, I found myself utterly unprepared for the scenes to which I was exposed as Holmes and I mingled with the unfortunates of Spitalfields that night.

God knows, they were pathetic creatures! On their faces one could see limned every last extreme of illness, deprivation, hopelessness, and vice. It was impossible to hazard a guess at their ages. I asked one, who looked older than the city itself. She told me that she thought she might be thirty-two, and then made a suggestion so indescribably filthy that I cannot bring myself to set it down. I was to hear many more such expressions that night but I never grew hardened to them. During my spell in Afghanistan I occasionally overheard talk in the mess concerning the abominable practices of some of the heathen superstitions, but never in my life had I expected to hear such language on the lips of an Englishwoman, however reduced in circumstances. I believe, however, that the greater number of the unfortunates in Whitechapel at that time were not in fact English at all, but of Celtic or Continental origin.

As Holmes and I moved ever deeper into this labyrinth of sin, it began to seem that we had been mysteriously spirited out of London and set down in some limbo inhabited by alien beings. We found ourselves continually the objects of immoral propositions, and since Holmes thought it expedient to question the women and to warn them, we were unable to dismiss these with the contempt they so richly merited. We had to stop, to listen, to look. And while my friend questioned the women verbally, I for my part tried to read the riddle of their faces. Ever since first hearing about the Whitechapel murders I had, like everyone else, envisaged the victims as being people of my own kind. One reads an empty name—Annie Chapman, or Elizabeth Stride—and fills in the features of the women one sees every day. It is a natural trick of the mind. But now, face to face with the type of the Ripper's prey, I found any such identification both impossible and absurd. Whatever else one might feel about these hags, one thing was absolutely clear—they were not as other women, or even as other people. Rather they were another species altogether. To my amazement and dismay, I found that the moral fury with which I had burned on learning of Moriarty's atrocities was now sensibly subsiding under a choking layer of cold indifference. I found myself posing terrible and unanswerable questions. What did it matter? What difference did it make whether the Ripper picked on this one, or that, or none, or all of them? No one would miss them. No one would care. No one—not even themselves—would regret their passing. Most were already dying by degrees of disease and inanition, and the Ripper's knife would be infinitely quicker and more merciful than the agonies that would attend their natural deaths.

Such were my thoughts, such the grim message I read in those battered features where nothing lived but the blind unreasoning instinct to go on living, even though life could mean nothing but pain.

It was past one when we returned, cold and weary, to the police station. My leg was starting to trouble me, and I was glad to be able to rest by the fire with a warm drink. Holmes had grown increasingly taciturn as our patrol had continued. Now he sat sullenly at the table, studying the plan affixed to the wall. At length I went over to join him. One odd thing I had noticed was that throughout our wanderings in Spitalfields we had hardly encountered a single policeman. I attempted to question my friend about this, but he only murmured something about 'the open door of the trap'. Lestrade, meanwhile, was as voluble as Holmes was reticent. He harped on and on in a carrying voice about the waste of time and money caused by this fruitless patrolling, and opined that such was invariably the result when pen-pushers started meddling in the affairs of the police. To all of this the assembled detectives added their vociferous assent. Suddenly Holmes sprang to his feet, took his coat and hat and walked out. I hurried after him, but he was moving so quickly that we were in the street before I caught up to him. To my chagrin he attempted to repulse me.

'Stay behind, Watson! I can see your leg is giving you pain.'

'It's nothing. I am quite used to it by now.'

'But I really have no need of you, my dear fellow. Must I be blunt? You can be of no assistance.'

But I was not to be put off this time.

'I am coming, Holmes, and that is final! If you think for one minute that I could sit there listening to Lestrade and drinking tea, while you are out here facing—'

'Oh very well then. Suit yourself. But we must make haste! Moriarty is already on the prowl. I can sense it!'

The wind whipped a light rain into our faces. Holmes

was walking at such a pace that I had the greatest difficulty in keeping stride with him. His eyes darted restlessly from side to side. His hands were tightly clenched and his whole frame seemed to tremble with agitation. Then, quite suddenly, he stopped dead in his tracks. He gazed into the darkness ahead of us. I looked, but I could see nothing remarkable. Then I realised that his fit was one of abstraction.

'Twice, Watson!' he said in a voice of quiet wonder. 'He must kill twice on the same spot!'

'What?'

'Ha! A pretty problem! This evening's victim, and the one we robbed him of last time. But he will have to kill them both on the same spot, or he throws his initial out. A pretty problem indeed!'

I paused to consider the question, but my companion was already yards away and moving almost at a run. I hurried after, but no sooner was I abreast of him than he once again pulled up short. We had reached a corner. A large church in the Classical style stood opposite, looking sadly out of place in this neighbourhood. Holmes's bony fingers encircled my wrist and pulled me back into the doorway of a public house. A moment later I heard the footsteps. Holmes's whisper was barely audible, yet I rocked on my feet as though he had struck me.

'It is he!'

The next instant a figure passed swiftly by our hiding-place. It was too dark for me to make out anything of his features, but by the same token Holmes and I escaped his notice. He crossed the road obliquely and disappeared into the street opposite without for a moment slackening his pace. As soon as he was out of sight, Holmes grasped my shoulders urgently.

'There's no time to lose!' he hissed. 'I will keep him in sight. Do you return to the station and alert Lestrade. He has his orders. But for God's sake hurry!'

With that he was gone. I am by no means clear about what happened next. The facts are plain enough—as I turned away to do Holmes's bidding my foot landed on the edge of the step on which we had been standing, wrenching my wounded ankle. The pain, though brief, was intense. When it passed I set off with all the speed I could muster. But instead of making for the police station, I went after Holmes and Moriarty. My decision deliberately to ignore the orders I had been given was completely spontaneous, and I would be hard put either to justify or explain it. Perhaps I had simply been deceived too many times lately by Holmes's stratagems, and had grown suspicious. At all events, my only thought now was to stick by my friend, whatever he was about. Moriarty might indeed be the devil incarnate, but I had no doubt he would stop a revolver bullet the same as any other man.

At Holmes's suggestion I had equipped myself with a pair of rubber-soled tennis shoes, and mine was thus a soundless progress along the dreary streets. I kept my eyes fixed on the pavement before me. My wound still throbbed uncomfortably, and another such mishap would incapacitate me for several minutes at least. As I reached the next corner I glanced up, only to find that Holmes had vanished from sight. Moriarty I could just make out as he passed beneath a lamp, walking straight ahead towards Bishopsgate. To my right rose the walls of the market. Looking to my left, I was astonished to see Holmes's tall figure hurrying towards the next street. Even as I watched he turned the corner, so that he was now headed back in the direction we had come. Utterly mystified, I hastened after him. The street, however, once I reached it, proved to be empty but for three vagrants perched on the kerb swilling beer from a can. I tried to collect my scattered wits. Even at a run, Holmes could not have gained Commerical Street again before I rounded the corner. He must therefore have entered one of the houses or courtyards in the street. But which one? And for what reason?

I had got myself into a fine mess with my brave initiative. Moriarty was lost to us, and now Holmes too had disappeared. For my part, I was faced with the choice of waiting there in the hope that Holmes might reappear, or returning contritely to the police station and enduring Lestrade's sarcasms. The latter prospect was sufficient to induce me to stay. I found a deeply recessed doorway in which to conceal myself, and crouched down there. It was a relief to take the weight off my leg, and my refuge was out of the wind. For a minute or two I sat there quite content. Then a very unpleasant thought struck me. What if Holmes had perceived that he was being followed? Would he not naturally assume that his pursuer was one of Moriarty's accomplices? Might he not slip down to the next street, enter a house, pass over the wall into the adjoining property, and thence regain the other street in safety, leaving the professor's ruffian to mark down an empty house? It seemed exactly the style of thing Holmes would be likely to do, whereas to abandon the chase for no apparent reason was utterly foreign to his nature. I had virtually convinced myself that this was indeed the true state of affairs, when I heard a door shut close by. I peered out. Some three or four houses back, a man had stepped out on to the pavement. I quickly pulled my head in again as he turned towards me. His soft footfall neared. There was a lodging-house adjacent, and as he passed his face caught the light from its lamp. I almost gave the game away then and there by my sharp intake of breath. The face was familiar. The man was Holmes.

The face was familiar and yet quite strange. Had I not been half-expecting to see my friend, I doubt I would have known him. He was a master of disguise, of course, but this one, like all great inspirations, was simplicity itself. He had darkened his complexion slightly, and added a fine moustache, curled at the tips. The effect was to give his face a distinctly Semitic appearance. This was accentuated by his dress, which might best be described as elegantly sumptuous. He wore a dark felt hat and a long fur-trimmed coat, beneath which I caught sight of a white collar and black tie retained from his original costume. He had a pair of kid gloves in one hand and a small package in the other, and carried himself in such a way as to appear a good six inches shorter than his full height. The general impression was of a prosperous man of commerce, 'something in the City', whose tastes still smacked of the bazaars and counting-houses from which his forefathers had come. It was a truly masterful impersonation, for he had not tried to impose alien features on his own by dint of trickery. Rather, with a few deft touches, he had exposed an alien Holmes, one I had never before seen, but who now seemed to have been there all the while in that face I had come to think of as so characteristically and essentially British.

This instant of recognition was succeeded by an acute sensation of doubt as to my own position. My natural impulse was to run after Holmes, confess my wrongheadedness, and throw myself on his mercy. I quickly thought better of this, however. These were deep waters, and it was by no means certain that Holmes would welcome my presence in them. On the other hand, I could hardly go off and abandon him. What if the message I was to have given Lestrade formed a vital element in his calculations? He had spoken of these unpatrolled streets as 'the open door of the trap'. Had my message been the signal to close that door? I began to appreciate how horribly short-sighted my insubordination had been. Had Holmes not praised me for my soldierly dependability, for my readiness to follow orders without question? What a hideous irony it would be if my failure in that respect proved his undoing! But it was too late now for second thoughts. All I could do was to follow my friend discreetly, and stand ready to lend such aid as I could if the need arose.

Holmes was evidently in no hurry now, and I was able to keep pace with him quite easily. Before we had gone very far, however, it occurred to me that my very presence, even at a distance, might constitute a danger. Our association was well known to Moriarty, as was my appearance. Holmes had disguised himself to perfection, but what about me? I decided to attempt a little elementary camouflage. I pulled off my coat, turned it inside out, and put it on again. I then removed my necktie, placed it in my hat, and threw both over a wall. This was good, but it needed some finishing touch. I walked nearer to the kerb and pretended to slip, precipitating myself into the gutter. I then rolled from side to side, distributing the mud about my person, before rising unsteadily. To complete the picture I rubbed a handful of dirt down my face. The cold night resounded with peals of laughter from the trio of inebriates. I ignored them and resumed my progress with some pride in my ability to emulate Holmes's methods. No one now, I thought, would stop to question that I had merely started to celebrate the Lord Mayor's accession a little early.

The rain, which came and went all night, had largely emptied the streets. The bleak buildings rose up on either side as sheer and forbidding as cliffs of basalt. We might have been lost in some monstrous abyss through which the wind gusted and howled with the primal force of a mountain torrent. The guttering lamps provided just enough illumination to make the desolation of the scene fully apparent. On and on we walked through the streets we had earlier patrolled side by side. Holmes kept moving steadily ahead, never pausing in his stride, never looking back. I kept to the opposite pavement and hung back at every corner, but clearly my friend had no inkling that he was being followed.

We seemed to have been walking for an hour or more when we encountered the man and the girl. My wound was by this time giving me considerable pain, and it was only with difficulty that I was able to maintain Holmes's pace, moderate though this was. I was in fact wondering how much longer I would be able to keep up this relentless march, when all at once the situation changed dramatically. The first thing I noticed was that Holmes had stopped at a street corner. A moment later a man passed by in the cross-street. He was somewhat stout, and was shabbily dressed, with a 'wideawake' hat. I did not remark him particularly, for we had passed and been passed by many persons in the course of our promenade. Holmes stopped at the corner for a minute or two, and then turned to the right and disappeared. I hastened to reach the corner, and there beheld a strange scene. Walking towards Holmes was a young woman dressed in a dark skirt and a shawl. She was evidently a prostitute, although rather younger and more attractive than most specimens of that class we had encountered. She seemed a little the worse for drink, and her gait was unsteady. As she came up to Holmes I was astonished to see my friend place his hand upon her shoulder in familiar fashion. He then made some remark at which they both laughed. All this was indeed, a cause for wonder, but my attention was drawn elsewhere, for a little further along the street I spied the man who had passed by a minute earlier. This disreputable-looking individual had stationed himself under the lamp of a public house, from which vantage point he was keeping a surreptitious eye on my friend and the young woman. Suddenly the affair began to assume a distinctly sinister aspect. Was it indeed by sheer coincidence that the man and the girl had happened to pass one another at this spot? Why had the man remained? Why was he showing such a marked interest, in a district where indifference was a cardinal virtue, in matters that were none of his business? Even as these thoughts were running through my head, Holmes and the young woman moved off together. As they passed by the watcher under the lamp I saw him look closely at Holmes, as if to make sure of his man. Then, as the couple turned the corner, he left his post to follow them.

I now had no further doubts. The man and the girl were clearly accomplices of Moriarty. Her task must be to lure Holmes to a suitably secluded spot where the man could strike him down. What a hideous accomplishment if this fell plan were to succeed! How Moriarty would gloat! What a brilliant exclamation mark to set to his gory monogram! But the game was not yet lost. The Professor's henchman had not observed my presence in the shadows, and while he stalked Holmes, I in turn marked him down. I was armed and ready, and my intervention would be all the more effective for being unexpected. Thus, in solemn procession, we passed through the gloomy corridors of Whitechapel. In the van was Holmes with the young woman, unaware that twenty yards back the stout man was skulking along on his trail, while the latter was in turn blissfully ignorant that bringing up the rear was one whose head was clear—despite appearances to the contrary—and whose untrembling fingers grasped the trigger of a loaded revolver. In this fashion we returned to the same squalid street from which I had followed Holmes in the first place. He and the girl came to rest at an archway between two houses. The stout man also stopped. On the other side of the street I stepped into a gateway from which I was able to command an excellent view of the proceedings. To anyone acquainted with the character of Sherlock Holmes, these were quite startling. The woman stood up against the arch, addressing him in the vulgar and piercing tone of her ilk. It was my friend's response which astonished me. His words were inaudible, but I plainly saw him lean forward and kiss the woman's face! They continued to converse together for a minute or two, before going in under the arch together. At once the stout man shook off his lethargy and marched boldly up to the archway. He looked into the passage, then he too vanished from sight.

Here, then, was the crisis! The girl had somehow induced Holmes to enter a dark alley, where the stout man was now about to assault him—no doubt striking the first blow while my friend's back was turned. There was not a moment to lose! I made for that archway with all the speed I could muster, given the state of my throbbing Achilles' tendon. But in the event it was as well I was not swifter, for as I was on the point of entering the passage I caught the sound of someone coming out. No sooner had I flattened myself in the doorway of the adjacent house than the stout man reappeared! He looked briefly up and down the street, and then proceeded to cross over to the lodging-house opposite, beneath whose lamp he took up his position as before.

I now had to revise my ideas. Evidently the ruffian was not himself going to attempt Holmes's life. His job was merely to keep watch, pending the arrival of some third party. It was no extraordinary feat of deduction to conclude that this would prove to be none other than Moriarty himself. The Professor was coming to settle accounts in person with his arch-enemy. Of course! It was absurd to think that at this supreme climax to the most audacious series of killings in history Moriarty would permit another the privilege of striking the fatal blow! He would come himself! He must come! This being the case, it only remained for me to gain entrance to the passage and warn Holmes of the danger in which he stood, and we might yet turn the tables on this inhuman genius. But how was I to get by the watchdog? For a moment I thought of simply drawing my revolver and taking the man in charge, but it soon occurred to me that it would not do for Moriarty to see that his Cerberus was missing. That would alert his suspicions, and he might make good his escape. How was I to manage it? I turned the question over in my mind without arriving at any conclusion. In the end, chance smoothed the way for me. A man came down the street and turned into the lodging-house. As he did so he caught sight of the stout man, with whom he was evidently acquainted. The two fell into conversation, in the course of which my adversary turned away, allowing me to slip from cover and enter the narrow vaulted passage. Once inside, the darkness wrapped me in a cloak of invisibility.

The alley led into a small unlit courtyard consisting of two rows of mean cottages facing each other across a gutter. I was wondering which of these dwellings might contain Holmes and the girl, when I was greatly startled to hear my friend's voice, seemingly at my elbow. I then noticed for the first time a door set in the wall to my right. Again I heard Holmes speak, although I could not make out the sense. I moved stealthily around the corner of the house, and soon discovered that it was possible to see through a chink in the curtains covering one of the two windows. I peered in.

The room was very small and cramped, although it contained only the barest modicum of furniture. A candle on the table before the window provided the only light. A mass of wood and coal was piled unlit in the grate. Some clothes lay scattered at the foot of the bed, upon which the female sprawled tilting a spirit-flask to her lips.

'Don't down it like blue ruin, woman!'

The voice was Holmes's. He was seated in the only chair in the room, his back to the window. The girl stared at him for a moment, her head swaying in befuddled puzzlement.

'You want some?' she asked finally.

Holmes had taken a snuffbox from his pocket, and was shaking the powder on to the back of his wrist. I was surprised at this, for I had never known him to take snuff. He drew the powder up into his nostrils, and then shook his head and laughed.

'No, I have rarer pleasures. "I am fire and air; my other elements I give to baser life." I meant only to point out that what you are drinking is fine cognac, not max at three-halfpence a measure.'

The woman shrugged and tossed the flask down on the bedcovers.

'It all goes the same way home, don't it?' said she with a giggle.

Just then I heard footsteps in the passage. My heart raced. Was Moriarty already upon us? I waited tensely, my back to the wall. Then the figure passed by and I saw that it was only an old woman. She disappeared into one of the cottages further down the yard. A false alert, but it had served to remind me how exposed was my position at the window. Anyone leaving the courtyard could not fail to see me there, and the resulting alarm might well ruin everything. Either I had to enter the room and warn Holmes, or conceal myself somewhere in the yard and await developments. After a moment's consideration I chose the second course. I found a spot for my bivouac at the end of the yard. From there I had a clear view of the only door to the room in which Holmes was waiting. The light rain had returned, but to an old campaigner the hardships of the post were slight and easily endured. I settled down with my back to the wall and my coat wrapped around me, basking in the inner satisfaction of knowing that for the first time since disobeying Holmes's original order I was once again in control of events. My friend was in no present danger, and I was well placed to challenge any future threat. I felt deeply relieved at having brought the affair to this happy stage.

I was deceived, of course, but it is not of that I am now ashamed. My errors were honest, and the truth an inconceivable abomination. No, what I blush to confess is my unforgivable weakness in falling asleep on my watch. For this there can be no excuse. Even if my conjectures had been correct it would have been a monstrous dereliction of duty. And who shall say what might have happened had I been awake to hear that voice that cried murder? But enough! The facts are that after lying huddled in the corner of that yard for over an hour, my body aching and my brain exhausted, I simply dozed off.

I awoke chilled to the bone, from what I thought at first to have been only a brief nap. I was aghast to discover on consulting my watch, that it was almost five o'clock! For a moment I lay incredulous on the cobbles where I had slumbered for close on two hours! Then, with a thrill of mortal terror, I remembered where I was. Holmes's words suddenly echoed through my skull. 'He must kill twice on the same spot!' Two victims: Holmes and the young woman! What could be simpler or more effective? It would be a typically economical and elegant solution to the 'pretty problem' my friend had mentioned. Moriarty would at once put an end to his duel with Holmes and dispose of a witness who might otherwise embarrass him in the future, while still fulfilling the requirements of his diabolical design.

I struggled to my feet and moved silently and swiftly up the courtyard to the window through which I had earlier spied on the room. To my chagrin I found the

curtains were now tightly drawn. Then I was stunned to
hear someone moving inside the room! I struggled to
control my excitement as I realised that though I might
be too late to save my friend, I could still avenge him.
As I edged cautiously around the corner towards the
door I noticed that one of the panes of the other window had been broken, and then crudely stopped up with
a piece of cloth. Here was a capital opportunity to re-
connoitre before launching my attack. With infinite care
I worked the wadding loose. Then I inserted my hand
and parted the curtains.

I was prepared for horrors, but for the sight that met
my eyes there could be no preparation. At first glance it
suggested some appalling natural disaster. Was it possible, I wondered, for a person to explode? Then, with
sickening certainty, I recognised this mess of strewn
flesh as the woman I had seen drinking and talking with
Sherlock Holmes a few hours before. He was still with
her, but not dead. No, much worse than dead. He was
alive. Stripped to his undergarments, he seemed a giant
in that tiny room. The fire was blazing and his shadow
moved hugely over the bed and its monstrous cargo. His
clothes had been neatly folded and piled in the chair,
safe from the gore that covered his hands and wrists
and arms and was spattered over his linen. As he moved,
so did his shadow, and then one saw more of the girl.
She lay on her back on the blood-drenched bed. Her
torso was completely flayed and gutted. The bed-table
was covered with her organs. Her arm had been sliced
through at the shoulder, and her hand shoved deep into
the shambles of her abdomen. Her gaping throat was a
horror to behold, but the worst by far was her face. The
nose had been ripped away, together with the ears, the
skin was cut to ribbons, but a devilish discretion had
saved her eyes. Undisturbed, they stared at me from out
of the wreckage of her face—a look as impossible to
avoid as it was to meet.

As for Holmes, he had his clay pipe and his pathologist's knife, and just then he was working on the right
thigh, stripping back the flesh to expose the femur.

After a while he laid down the knife, lifted a piece of meat and arranged it carefully to hang from the picture-rail. He hummed a sprightly melody as he worked. I could not place it at the time, but having heard the piece since in rather different circumstances I am able to reveal, for what it may be worth, that it is known as 'La donna é mobile'.

# Four

As an army surgeon, I saw much of men who had sustained massive physical injuries. Those most severely wounded, strangely enough, are often the quietest. The screaming and the writhing are characteristic of the less critical cases. The most grievous seem to be protected from the full awareness of their plight; a merciful trance descends upon their senses, and if they subsequently recover they are very often unable to remember anything material from the period when their lives were despaired of. I cannot help feeling that something of this sort must have happened to me at the moment I am describing, although in my case it was the spirit rather than the flesh which had received the mortal blow. At all events, I find myself quite unable to recount in any detail the manner in which I spent that holiday Friday. All I can recall are a few vivid impressions, lacking all sense and sequence. My memory, like an idiot messenger, has forgotten all the vital items, while retaining trivia of no interest or importance. Thus I possess a clear memory of sitting on a form in a poky room lit by two oil lamps so filthy that they seemed rather to absorb light than to give it out. I stayed there for I know not how long, downing glass after glass of some liquid which the old hag behind the bar described as gin, though it tasted more like medicinal spirits. After that I am at a loss again. Where did I go? What did I do? It seems I fell on some wet tram-lines and lay helpless for several minutes together on the cobbles. Later, I think, I tried to board a cab, but the driver, no doubt dismayed by my appearance, cut at me with his whip. There were crowds everywhere by then, and bells pealing, and a procession with bands and horses and men dressed up as if for an old play, while urchins rushed past screaming about a horrible murder and people whispered together with fear in their eyes. Then all is blank.

I came to my senses lying face down under a rose bush. The sky was dark and a strong wind was blowing. I felt shaky, but myself again. A row of lights indicated that a broad thoroughfare passed close by. A tall pillar rose into the stormy darkness, and I heard again the mournful whistle of the steam launch which had awakened me. The pillar I recognised as that obelisk popularly known as Cleopatra's Needle. With some difficulty I climbed the railings and dropped to the pavement. I stood for a moment under a lamp, inspecting my appearance. It was not reassuring. To discover himself, lying in a flowerbed in a public gardens, without the slightest notion of how he came to be there, must prove an embarrassment to any respectable person. The case is by no means improved when he discovers that his hat, his tie, his money and his watch are all missing, that he is wearing his coat inside-out, that his other clothes are all wet and filthy, and that his shirtfront smells distinctly of cheap gin.

By turning my coat the right way again I was able to conceal the worst of my condition, and when a hansom passed by a few minutes later I was able to get myself accepted as a fare after a short parley with the driver. When he enquired as to my destination I replied unthinkingly 'Baker Street', and at one stroke the memory of what I had witnessed that morning came howling back into my mind. How was I to face Holmes? The thing was impossible. But I was penniless and completely unpresentable. Moreover, if I did not quickly change into some dry clothes I stood a very good chance of developing pneumonia. What was I to do? 221B or not 221B? That was the question, and by the time the cab had reached Baker Street I had arrived at an answer. I directed the cabbie to drive on to the corner of King Street,* and then to run back and see if Mr Holmes was at home. This he did, after some promised bribery. If Holmes was there I had determined to brave the stares at my club. But I was in luck. My jarvey brought good tidings, for which he was duly rewarded, and in a few minutes I was brushing off Mrs Hudson's expressions of alarm while gratefully accepting her offer of a bath followed by something hot and nourishing. She had seen nothing of her other lodger, it appeared, but there was a telegram for me on the table in the hall. I read the wire as I climbed the stairs. It had been dispatched from Dover that afternoon, and ran this way:

M got by us in Whitechapel but I have picked up his trail. He is seeking to escape to the Continent but he shall not escape me. Hold your ground and await further dispatches. Holmes.

Relieved as I was to learn that Holmes's absence was to continue for some time, his cable only intensified the mystery. I read it through once more. It was, beyond a doubt, the voice of the Holmes I had always known—a man quite incapable of the atrocities I had nevertheless watched him committing that very morning. For a moment I began to wonder if I could be losing my mind. Two equally strong and valid truths were firmly lodged

*Now part of Blandford Street.

in that organ, and unfortunately for its continuing welfare they contradicted one another. The first was that I had seen Holmes coolly mutilating the body of a dead woman. The second was that Holmes was Holmes, and such a thing was therefore impossible.

I pushed this dilemma aside while I had my bath, changed, and ate the ample fare provided by Mrs Hudson. But once my immediate needs had been taken care of the larger question returned in full force and would no longer be denied. I reconsidered the matter, inclining first one way and then the other. No sooner had I convinced myself that Holmes was himself the Whitechapel murderer and his tale of Professor Moriarty all a blind, than all my instincts rose up and threw out such a preposterous notion. But then the memory of that barbaric scene returned, and I no longer knew what to think. Was it possible I had dreamt the entire episode? If so, the consequences for myself must be very serious, for I would have lost the use of my reason. But would it be any easier to admit that my best friend, my honoured mentor, with whom I had lived on terms of the greatest intimacy for more than seven years, was a maniacal homicide?

At length I realised that certain aspects of my morning's experience could be checked. If there had been a murder, it would have been reported in the papers. I assembled the great mass of newsprint which Holmes had delivered to our rooms daily, and sat down to sift through it. There seemed to be nothing to the point in the morning papers, and for a moment my sanity seemed to hang in the balance. But of course the reason was simply that the body had not been discovered until late morning. In the evening editions I soon found what I was looking for. The victim was believed to have been one Mary Kelly, twenty-four years old. The murder had taken place in Miller's Court, an alley off Dorset Street. The body had been mutilated in a manner surpassing description. There could be no doubt that Jack the Ripper had struck again, and with a ferocity and daring that eclipsed even his previous outrages.

I was still reading these reports when the bell rang. It was ten past eleven. Holmes used to say that after eleven o'clock callers were invariably either criminals or policemen. In this case, it proved to be the latter. I opened the door to Inspector Lestrade, who pushed past me with an assurance that comes with years of paying official visits.

'Good evening, Doctor. I hope you don't mind me calling so late, but I saw your lamp was lit. I was wanting a word with Mr Holmes.'

I hardly knew what to say. Had the police then discovered already what I still could not bring myself to believe?

'Holmes? Oh yes, Holmes. Ah! No. He's not in. That's to say, he's out. Away, I should say—'

But Lestrade had already spotted the buff form, which he picked up and read without compunction.

'Hm. Off to the Continent, is he? Well, well!'

He looked up at me with a slight sneer. I determined to brazen it out.

'It will be well indeed, if he succeeds in running this fiend to earth.' I declared roundly. 'We at least have not come away utterly empty-handed, Inspector. What about you?'

'Well I certainly can't go running off to Gay Paree the moment things go wrong, if that's what you mean,' growled Lestrade. 'As for Mr Holmes's precious charts and timetables, I've had a bellyful of them!'

I felt immensely reassured. This was the old Lestrade, and he clearly suspected nothing.

'Come now,' I rallied him, 'you cannot deny that Holmes predicted the murderer's attack with complete accuracy.'

The detective sneered. 'So he did, Dr Watson, so he did. Unfortunately it wasn't his fortune-telling we were interested in so much as catching the Ripper. We weren't quite so successful there, were we? Mr Holmes had Whitechapel packed with policemen, all except one little area in Spitalfields. And that's where our Jack walked in, did his business, and got clean away again, while we were all cooling our heels at the police station. Well I was, at any rate. I don't know what became of you two.'

I avoided this question by offering Lestrade a drink, which he readily accepted. Then, assuming that I was quite ignorant of what had happened, he began to describe the scene of the murder.

'The funny thing is, it all happened in the very same street that Mr Holmes has his room, where I sent for him the last time. Right under his very nose, in Dorset Street. "Do as you please", they call it around there, and that's what the murderer did all right. I've never seen anything like it. He'd locked the door somehow, and we had to take out the window to get inside. And let me tell you, it's just as well I'd had my lunch before I went down there, for it'll be a good few days before I have a stomach for meat again. You have no idea what that poor girl looked like, Doctor, and you may thank your lucky stars you don't. It's a sight a man would never forget if he lived to be a hundred. That's what people don't understand when they go on at the police. No one wants this devil locked up worse than we do. God only knows what he'll dream up to cap this, but one thing is sure—we're the ones who are going to have to go down and look at it.'

For a minute or two we sat silently thinking our separate thoughts. Then, almost inaudibly, Lestrade began again.

'That's not the worst of it, either. We had to keep it from the press, but it can't hurt to tell you. There is one final horror.'

'What can be worse than this?'

'The girl was pregnant.'

'My God.'

'Three months gone, and her womb cut up like cat's-meat.'

I felt an icy finger touch my spine.

' "He must kill twice on the same spot!" '

'What was that?'

'Oh, nothing of importance. But tell me, what paths of enquiry are you following?'

The detective laughed hollowly.

' "Paths of enquiry"? What paths? There are no paths. No one saw him come, no one saw him go. One old whore heard someone cry out, and then went back to sleep. In Dorset Street folk screaming and yelling is like the birds singing down in Kent. What are we supposed to do? We're not second-sighted, you know.'

'Did the killer leave no clue to his identity?'

'There was a clay pipe, but it might have belonged to anyone. I don't think the girl was too particular about the company she kept, if you take my meaning. Apart from that there was just some female clothing and the furniture, unless he burned something in the fireplace. Funny thing that—the ashes were still warm when we got in there. He must have had quite a blaze going, and I can't see why. Something like that could attract attention, which you'd think would be the last thing he'd have wanted.'

I gestured languidly, as Holmes was wont to do.

'I see no great problem there, my dear fellow. The murderer no doubt lit the fire for the usual excellent reasons. It was none too warm this morning—outside the police station, at any rate—and if the killer removed his outer garments before mutilating the body, as I presume he must, then he would certainly have wished to heat the room. Besides, he would have needed the extra illumination. One cannot perform a satisfactory dissection, even of a crude nature, by the light of a single candle.'

I smiled at Lestrade, who was staring at me curiously.

'A candle?' said he. 'Did I say anything about a candle?'

It was an uncomfortable moment.

'Well, my dear Lestrade! Ha! I mean, surely one may assume with some confidence that such a hovel as the papers describe is unlikely to have the gas laid in? What?!'

The official gazed at me blankly. Then he shook his head, as if to clear it, and rose from his chair.

'That's what this job does to you,' he complained. 'The next thing you know I'll be suspecting you, Doctor! Ha ha!'

'Ha, ha, ha!'

'Ha ha! Oh, that's rich! Well, thank you kindly for the refreshment. I won't keep you up any longer. Give Mr Holmes my best wishes for his Grand Tour. Who is this M, anyway?'

'Oh, that's just a cipher. He means "the murderer".'

'Ah yes, of course. Well good night.'

I sat up for a full hour after Lestrade left, reflecting on what he had told me, and what I already knew, and what I thought I knew, but without finding any way out of my quandary. In the morning I renewed my efforts, and eventually hammered out a solution that was to satisfy me for the next few days. It hinged on the fact that although I had seen Holmes disfiguring the woman's corpse, I had not seen him actually killing her. Might it not be that the mutilation, on the face of it so damning, was in truth a necessary part of Holmes's plan for trapping the real killer—Professor Moriarty? Suppose Holmes had been unable to prevent the Miller's Court murder, but had seen a way of bringing the killer to justice. Suppose this involved mutilating the corpse to a degree undreamed of even by the Professor. If this were the case, my friend's sternly unemotional nature would not have faltered. He would have weighed the greater good against the lesser evil, and done whatever was needful. It was true I could by no means see how the extent of the victim's injuries could possibly affect the capture of her killer. But then Holmes's designs were habitually far beyond my understanding. At any rate, this explanation provided a reasonable and characteristic key to a set of circumstances which otherwise seemed inexplicable.

For a few days, as I have said, this theory satisfied me, but a time came when I had to admit it would no longer do. On Thursday, the 15th of November, I received a telegram from Berne in Switzerland, which read as follows: 'M is no more. Returning Saturday. Holmes.' This terse message plunged me into a condition approaching panic. Holmes was returning! Holmes would be arriving in two days! But was it Holmes I would see walking in through the door? Was it Holmes's sinewy hand I would grasp, or the incarnadine paw of Jack the Ripper? Could I sit down before the fire and smoke a pipe and exchange pleasantries with a man who might be the Whitechapel murderer? No! The thing was unthinkable. It was no longer enough for me simply to give my friend the benefit of the doubt. I had to know the truth—and quickly!

Back in 1881, shortly after moving into 221B Baker Street, I had devoted an idle moment to drawing up a list of my new companion's personal traits, as I then understood them, hoping thereby to deduce the line of work in which he was engaged. This prosaic method must be congenial to my disposition, for seven years later I once again had recourse to it. But my 'little list' was this time of a decidedly more sinister cast. I worked at it until the winter dusk descended outside, and then I lit the lamp and worked on. At last I felt sure that I had overlooked nothing of importance. Here is the memorandum I had drawn up:

Could Sherlock Holmes have committed the Whitechapel murders?
PRO:
1 Holmes was in Whitechapel on the night of the double killing, and of this latest horror, and in each case he was alone at the requisite times.
2 On the other hand, when he was occupied with other work in October, and that weekend when I stuck with him every minute (despite his protests), there were no deaths.
3 As for the earlier murders, my diary shows that Holmes was out on the night of August 30th-31st. Of August 6th-7th and September 7th-8th I have no record.

4 Like Holmes, the killer is evidently a master of disguise, since witnesses' descriptions of him differ widely.

5 The killer is able to mutilate a human body quickly and thoroughly, working almost in the dark. He can locate even such inaccessible organs as the kidney. This indicates a sound training in practical anatomy, which was one of the subjects Holmes studied at Bart's.

6 It is agreed that the killer must be intimately familiar with every alley and courtyard in Whitechapel. No one knows this or any other district of London better than Holmes.

7 After the Mitre Square murder the trail led by way of Goulston Street to Dorset Street, where, I now learn, Holmes's Whitechapel bolt-hole is situated.

8 Holmes could have made the writing in Goulston Street. The forged letter he sent Lestrade at the end of last month proves his mastery of the hand. (And was it in fact a calf's kidney he used to smear my calling card with blood?)

9 One great mystery is how the killer continues to elude the police patrols. This would be no great feat for Holmes, since it is he who plans their timetable in the first place.

CONTRA:

1 Holmes is above all a great champion of the law— *the* great champion. It is unthinkable that he could be a party to, much less a prime mover of, such a monstrous series of criminal acts.

2 I have lived with this man for seven years. He is no more a murderer than I am, and that is all there is to it.

Reading through this summary proved a sobering experience. I was amazed to find so much evidence suggesting that Holmes was indeed guilty, and even more shocked to discover no single unequivocal fact that proved his innocence. The case for the prosecution was no doubt purely circumstantial, and any given item by itself might mean little enough. But taken together it had all the force of 'a trout in the milk', and when one added the evidence I had gathered with my own eyes that morning in Miller's Court, it amounted to a very weighty indictment. And what could the defence produce by way of a reply? Nothing but my own testimony as a character witness; my conviction that Holmes was simply not capable of these monstrous atrocities.

Once I saw that this was the case, I naturally started to wonder just how well-founded this conviction of mine was. Not that I wished to undermine it, but if my understanding of Holmes's character was all that stood between me and the possibility that I was sharing rooms with Jack the Ripper, I needed to test its foundations rigorously. For the remainder of that evening, therefore, I sat down and examined, as coldly and impersonally as I could, everything that I knew about Sherlock Holmes. I tried to put aside all my fixed and cherished beliefs, and to examine Holmes as though I were meeting him for the first time. The results of this exercise were startling. In the end, I found that almost everything I had come to take for granted about Holmes was at best highly questionable and at worst transparently false.

Where did this leave the case for the defence? The first of its two arguments had been that Holmes was 'above all a great champion of the law—*the* great champion'. Previously, this had always seemed self-evident. Holmes had devoted his life to bringing criminals to justice. To question whether he was a champion of the law seemed on the face of it as absurd as to enquire whether the Archbishop of Canterbury was a Christian. It was of course true that on more than one occasion, having discovered the guilty party, he had summarily appointed himself judge and jury, and allowed a murderer to die in freedom, or a thief to flee the country. But these were only trivial infractions—one might even say, liberal interpretations—of the great rule. The rule itself still obtained. Or did it? As I thought about it, I came to see that for a champion of the law, Holmes's manner of going about his work was, to say the least, eccentric. When it was a question of accepting or rejecting a case, did he listen to his supplicant's tale of woe with the feeling that a wrong had been done which it was his duty to put right? Hardly. Moral fervour was a luxury Holmes allowed himself only after having ascertained that the problem presented the necessary features of interest. That was the criterion by which all pleas were judged, and if the case did not interest him he would have nothing to do with it. Was that the approach of a champion of the law, or of a profoundly abstract intellect, which found in criminal investigation an arena for the exercise and display of certain skills? The answer became clear when I considered that, for a true champion of the law, Utopia would be a land where criminal acts were unknown. To Holmes, such a region would truly deserve the legend: 'All hope abandon, ye who enter here.'

Once I had grown somewhat accustomed to seeing him in this novel light, I asked myself how I could ever have been so utterly mistaken about Holmes. But the answer was obvious enough. As a chess player must choose first of all the white pieces or the black, so Holmes, in his search for intellectual challenge, had chosen to side with the forces of the law. And since he manipulated them so well, we had all come to identify Holmes with the white pieces—as if their fate meant anything to him outside the game. *The game!* That was his sole delight. And when it palled, when there were no longer any opponents worthy of his powers, he did not rejoice at the overthrow of the black counters. No, he fretted and sulked, and plunged himself into a world of artificial stimulation. There it was, no doubt, in some dark and dismal cavern of the mind unlocked by the spells of cocaine, that a voice had prompted him to move to the other side of the board. It should have come as no surprise to me, of all people. How many times had I heard him bemoan the dullness and lack of enterprise of the criminal class? How many times had he muttered darkly that it was fortunate for society that he chose to spend his energies capturing felons rather than emulating them? How many times had I listened to his speculations on what he might be doing if it were his place to initiate a case instead of standing idly by until one was committed? All in all, it seemed inevitable that Sherlock Holmes should sooner or later have turned to crime.

This was all very well, as far as it went. But surely it did not go nearly far enough to account for the Whitechapel horrors. If Holmes's very own genius had driven him to crime, as I was now ready to believe, would not the basic humanity of the man have ensured that he confined his operations to crimes against property? Here at any rate I could make my stand. The entire fabric of insinuations and innuendo must fall before the simple declaration I had noted down as my second objection to this monstrous charge—Holmes was not a murderer. Amoral he might be; above the law he might consider himself; a criminal he might even become, but a killer he was not. That, as I had written, was all there was to it.

If the matter had been less pressing I would have been content to leave it thus. But the news of Holmes's imminent return had put me to the question in no uncertain fashion. I could not afford the luxury of a suspended judgment. I had to decide whether or not I was to continue to live in Baker Street, and the decision could not be postponed. Yet again I strove to concentrate my mind. But I was too tired, and I could no longer focus my attention. I lay back in my chair and lit a cigarette. Midnight had struck, and it was now the morning of Friday the 16th. Seven days had passed since I stood petrified before that terrible tableau. Now the full horror of it seized my soul again, and like a boreal blast it swept away the fog that had been obscuring my vision of the truth. Suddenly, overwhelmingly, I knew! Holmes's manner—that was the key! All my sophistry fell to pieces as I recalled with chilling vividness not *what* I had seen Holmes do, but *how* he had done it. That relaxed deliberation! That air of a master admiring his handiwork! Sherlock Holmes incapable of murder? Nonsense! The man who could coolly flay and gut the body of a pregnant woman while whistling airs from Italian opera—though it be for the best reason in the world—was capable of anything and everything.

Thus far, in this trial *in camera,* I had relied exclusively on the form of argument I had learned from Holmes to call the inductive. Working from the facts as I knew them, I had tried to assess the probability of Holmes being the murderer. Now my vision of the scene in Miller's Court suggested another way. If my friend was capable of murder, what kind of murder would he be likely to commit? I could not imagine him killing anyone whose life was of the slightest value to mankind, or a source of pleasure to themselves or others. He would therefore choose for his victims those whose lives were brutal, brief, and beastly. Moreover, his legendary coldness to women made it marginally more likely that his victims would be female. Thus the evidence already suggested that he would seek his prey among the unfortunates of the East End. But there was a further clue, furnished by Holmes's character, which virtually clinched the matter. This was his almost pathological abhorrence of any reference to the act of which that class of female is but a walking incarnation. If he were to kill, therefore, he might well kill Whitechapel prostitutes. It was, after all, the absolute minimum murder— a mere step away from euthanasia.

And the mutilation? That, of course, followed of necessity once he had come thus far. For killing Whitechapel prostitutes would present no challenge to a man of Holmes's calibre. It was too easy. In order to make the game difficult and dangerous enough to be satisfying, he would have to handicap himself, and the best way of doing this would be to alert the press, the public, and the police to his intentions. But how was he to attract their attention in the first place? As Lestrade had complained, Whitechapel was a criminal's paradise. Violent death was an everyday occurrence there, and Holmes's murders, without embellishment, would have aroused no more public interest than a report of a dog-biting incident in Westminster. But if the same dog was savagely to maul several people in the same area, disappearing each time without trace, then the press would sit up and take notice. Thus Holmes had hit on his final tactics. After killing the unfortunates, he would gratuitously mutilate their remains and leave them in the street for the next passer-by to stumble on. The effect was all he could have desired. How strange it was, I thought, that the solution should hinge upon the idea of Holmes disfiguring the dead. One of the first things young Stamford had told me about Sherlock Holmes before he introduced us, back in 1881, was that he was in the habit of beating the subjects in the dissecting-rooms at Bart's with a stick. It all fitted together. I had come full circle.

On this positive note I fell asleep in my chair. When I awakened I found all my certainties in ruins again. Sherlock Holmes—my Holmes!—the face behind the Ripper's mask? In the cold light of dawn my conclusion seemed utterly fantastic, and the arguments which had led me to it had all fled. But I could no longer delay. I packed my meagre possessions into two trunks, and moved that very morning to an hotel. The same evening I summoned Mary to dine with me, unchaperoned. We had sherry with the soup, hock with the lobster, Beaune with the beef, and champagne with the soufflé. Over coffee I begged her to let us be married immediately. I explained with passionate insistence that I was finding it quite impossible to sleep soundly whilst these dreadful murders continued, knowing as I did that my all was living in a household bereft of any male defender. In vain Mary protested that respectable women were not threatened, that the scene of the crimes was Whitechapel and not Camberwell, and that the risk was therefore insignificant. I brushed aside these objections. How could she tell what such a maniac might do next? No one could deplore indecent haste more than I, but I could not help my tender feelings. As she had observed, I was looking unusually pale and strained. The remedy was in her hands. Not until the light of my life was safe under my own roof would I recover my health once more. At length she yielded to my importunate demands, and we parted on the understanding that our union would take place as soon as the necessary arrangements could be made.

The next morning I despatched a letter to 221B Baker Street. Although I could not face the prospect of meeting Holmes again, much less of sharing rooms with him, I had every reason for wishing to remain on good terms with my former friend. Rather than make a brutal severance, therefore, I bent the truth to suit my purposes. The letter ran this way:

My dear Holmes,

Much to my regret, I am unable to welcome you home in person. But I have a good excuse—the best in the world in fact! Mary and I have married. You will no doubt be somewhat surprised at the suddenness of the nuptials—indeed, I was myself! The fact is that poor Mary has been completely unnerved by these Whitechapel horrors. After the last atrocity she broke down altogether. As you know, there is no man in the Forrester household to exert a steadying influence, and between the two of them the women succeeded in convincing themselves that they were destined to be the murderer's next victims! Of course I pointed out that respectable women were not at risk and that in any case the scene of the crimes was invariably Whitechapel and not Camberwell. But you know how it is once the sex take an idea into their heads! Nothing would do but we must marry without further delay. I agreed, if only to remove Mary from the influence of this unhealthy morbidity. As for Mrs Forrester, I believe she has gone to stay with relatives in Yorkshire.

I am delighted to hear that you have been able to bring Professor Moriarty's career to a fitting end. If you have indeed ensured that these ghastly killings have reached their term, all England owes you its thanks. Naturally I am eager to have the details from your own lips. I sincerely hope that all the to-do that goes with setting up a household will not too long prevent me from satisfying this desire. By way of honeymoon, my wife and I are vagabonding it along the South Coast, spending a few days in each town. A letter to my club will reach me without undue delay.

Yours truly,
Watson

I posted this letter from Brighton, where I spent the next five days in seclusion. Counting on Mary's acquiescence, I had made arrangements for us to be married at a small church in Marylebone. I thought it best to spend the intervening days out of town, to avoid the possibility of an embarrassing encounter with Holmes. At the end of the following week Mary and I were duly united, and we left London that afternoon for the coast of Norfolk. Cromer is scarcely at its best in November, but it is very quiet. In that quiet, with Mary at my side, I found the strength to face and master the shocking truth on which I had so innocently stumbled.

I soon realised that although I had now resolved my immediate personal problems, I was still facing a very grave moral dilemma. I had reason to believe that Sherlock Holmes had committed six brutal murders, and might well attempt more. What was I to do? Under normal circumstances, of course, I would simply have informed the police. Such was indeed my duty, and by failing to do so I was myself breaking the law. But how could I possibly walk into a police station and announce that I believed the Whitechapel murderer to be a man celebrated throughout the world for his services in the fight against crime? Even supposing I was not at once clapped into a strait waistcoat, what evidence could I adduce in support of my wild accusation? Only some scraps of circumstantial minutiae that would not convict even a known criminal, together with my unsupported word that I had seen Holmes mutilating the body of Mary Kelly. And in any event, even if by some miracle

I did succeed in persuading the police to investigate a man they doubtless considered about as likely a suspect as the Prince of Wales, what would come of it? All the objections which Holmes had advanced when I proposed telling Lestrade about Professor Moriarty applied with equal force in the present case. The police could take no measures of which Holmes would not instantly be aware, and which he could not evade with the greatest of ease. The primary advantage we possessed was that Holmes had no reason to suppose that he was suspected. This advantage could hardly be overestimated, since it virtually cancelled out the man's natural superiority. As long as he did not exert his powers, he might yet be foiled, but if he were put on his guard it would be hopeless. Any resort to the authorities was therefore out of the question, for they were bound to bungle the affair.

But if I could not pass on my responsibilities to others, then I would have to shoulder them myself. Whatever my personal feelings, I would have to cultivate Holmes's friendship and keep a close watch on his moods and movements. And if he ever again took up his knife I would have to be there to fetch the police and hand the murderer over to justice. For a moment I even regretted the impulse that had made me leave the Baker Street rooms. My surveillance would have been much easier had I stayed. But at such close quarters Holmes must have remarked the change in my manner, and that would have been fatal. Besides, my task was by no means as arduous as it at first appeared, for if Holmes maintained the pattern which he had been at such pains to point out to Lestrade (How he must have amused himself! What fearful fun!) then the only times at which a close watch need be kept were the few days at the end of each month and at the weekend immediately following. It could be done and I had to do it. What I needed, therefore, was a residence close enough to Baker Street to make frequent 'dropping in' appear natural, and a practice sufficiently undemanding to free me for my larger duty—protecting the public from Jack the Ripper!

By now the end of November was drawing nigh, and with it the threat of another outrage. On the 28th I travelled back to London, leaving Mary safe in Cromer. My plan was to put up at an hotel for the weekend, but this was abruptly altered by a letter which I found awaiting me at the club. The envelope was addressed in a familiar hand, and the enclosure read as follows:

23rd November 1888

My dear Watson,

I read your communication of the 16th inst. with much interest, and with regret that my business in Switzerland made it impossible for me to attend your wedding. Please accept my best wishes for the future, and remember me kindly to your wife.

I fear that your eagerness to know more about the demise of the late and unregretted Professor Moriarty will have to be restrained for some time yet. The Russian Embassy has intimated that the Imperial authorities are prepared to offer me carte-blanche if I can shed any light on the mysterious case of a certain gentleman of Odessa. I know not who Mr Trepoff was, that the Czar's ministers should concern themselves with his fate, but the case possesses certain features of interest which in themselves induced me to accept. It seems the man was found seated at a desk in his hotel room with a volume of Lermontov's verse opened before him. There was no blood, no disorder. Indeed, the only indication of foul play was that the gentleman's head was missing. The one other occupant of the room was Trepoff's valet, who is apparently stark staring mad and unable to make any sound beyond a continuous series of farmyard imitations.

I depart for Odessa tomorrow, and whatever the outcome I expect to remain away from London for some time. Now that Jack the Ripper is gone I find the city 'stale, flat, and unprofitable'. I really cannot

bring myself to take any interest in the petty misde-
meanours of our insular criminals. Hopefully, the
Continental villain has not yet erased all traces of imagination and creativity from his work, but if he too
fails me I can at least purchase a Baedecker and a
sketch-book and turn tourist.

At all events, do not neglect to send word of your
address once you are settled. Mrs Hudson will forward all correspondence.

> Yours very truly,
> Sherlock Holmes

As I scanned these lines I experienced a relief that
was almost physical. Every phrase seemed to breathe
normality and to speak of the Holmes I had known and
respected for so long, rather than the fearsome monster
I had steeled myself to meet. Besides, I rejoiced to hear
that he was removing himself voluntarily from the
scenes that had witnessed those hideous outbursts of de-
structive violence. A period abroad might work a power
of good. It was with a serenity I had not known for
many weeks that I returned to Mary that evening, to
inform her that we could complete our honeymoon
without further interruption.

The hands of the clock which tells the time of my
narrative must now revolve more quickly. Three months
passed by. I acquired a modest practice in the Paddington district, and my days were spent quietly and use-
fully, attending to the ailments of my patients and to my
responsibilities as a husband and a householder. But I
am not penning my autobiography, and my only contact
with Sherlock Holmes during this period was through
the two typically vivid letters I received from him,
which I shall make no vain attempt to paraphrase. The
first was dispatched from Darjeeling, in Bengal, on the
4th of January. It ran:

Dear Watson,
    No doubt you have been wondering at my long si-
lence, but I have been travelling lately in parts not

noted for the regularity of their postal systems. Having cleared up the Odessa mystery I found, to my not complete amazement, that the cordiality of the Russian authorities had decidedly waned upon my discovering the identity of 'Mr Trepoff'. When four very large gentlemen visited my hotel room in the early hours of the morning, carrying a coffin, I felt that the time had come to take my leave. Fortunately I had detected the odour of cyanide of potassium in the champagne sent up by an anonymous admirer earlier in the evening (not that I care for sweet champagne in any case—they really should take the trouble to get these details right!) and was concealed in the chimney when the cortège called.

Using just about every form of transport known to man, and several previously unknown to me, I made my way through the Crimea and south to Baku. I then crossed the Caspian Sea and struck out into the great Kara Kum desert, from which I emerged, after a number of interesting incidents, in Afghanistan. The Russians were of course expecting me to head into the Balkans, or across the Black Sea into Turkey, and I was determined to disappoint them. It is no exaggeration to say that the information I now possess, if communicated to certain parties, could well result in the overthrow of the present régime in Russia. You will know how little interest I have in such an event, but one can hardly blame the Czar's men for preferring to guarantee my silence. I must therefore keep out of the way until next month, after which the matter will cease to be of any moment.

To while away the time, I have just spent a few days in Lhasa. One of the Viceroy's staff happened to mention in the course of conversation that no European had ever penetrated this 'forbidden city' of Tibet. I naturally need no further inducement. Well, it may still be true that no European has been there, but one very ancient and venerable Buddhist ascetic visited the Lama last month *en pèlerinage*, and had he removed his magnificent beard and expression of

transcendental sublimity, you might well have remarked his astonishing resemblance to

yours very truly,
Sherlock Holmes


This epistle was followed some three weeks later by
another, scarcely less singular, which had been written
at Colombo on the island of Ceylon:


Dear Watson,

I have, as you see, moved south, but for professional rather than personal reasons. A terrible tragedy has struck one of the leading families of these
parts, and the authorities, who are utterly baffled
(*Plus ça change* . . . !) have asked me to look into
it. I must admit that it appears to have the makings
of a very pretty little puzzle. I have not as yet begun
my investigation in person, but from what I gather
the protagonists were two brothers, Henry and Edward Atkinson, sole heirs to a large tea plantation
near Trincomalee, whither I am bound tomorrow. It
seems that Henry was playing cards at the Service
Club when his brother rushed in, shot Henry six
times with the greatest deliberation, and then calmly
gave himself up. Such an affair, on the face of it,
hardly seems to warrant my intervention—even poor
Lestrade might be forgiven for thinking the case cut
and dried. So indeed it seemed, until Henry's body
underwent a routine examination at the mortuary. It
was then discovered that his corpse was entirely unmarked by any lesion whatsoever, while his stomach
contained a quantity of poison which had been the
cause of death! Thus we presently have the interesting situation of Edward freely confessing to having
shot his brother, which brother however turns out not
to have been shot but poisoned—the whole affair
having taken place before a hundred eminent members of what passes here for society. A little *re-
cherché,* wouldn't you agree?

If I were in fact the calculating machine some people claim, I might well decide to postpone my return to England indefinitely. 'Go west, young man!' may be excellent advice to the morally upright, but the cream of the unrighteous, no doubt out of sheer perversity, seem to have gone east. As it is, though, I find that with every day that passes I yearn increasingly for the dreary fogs and familiar tedium of the London scene. I shall defend myself from any charge of irrationality by claiming that it is quite natural that I should wish to see for myself how my friend Watson is adapting to the rigours of domestic bliss. Need I say how much I am looking forward to seeing both you and Mrs Watson once more? I fear that your wife may not be well pleased with me for having so long tolerated your inherent bohemianism, but since I played a humble role in bringing the two of you together she may nevertheless feel able to receive, upon his return from our eastern dominions,

yours very truly,
Sherlock Holmes

A postscript, added two days later, ran this way:

My investigations here at Trincomalee have confirmed my initial conjectures regarding the Atkinson case. I do not expect to be detained here long—indeed, I should not arrive much later than this letter, unless something else comes up. Should one of your errands of mercy take you conveniently close to our old rooms you might have the goodness just to walk up and see that all is in order.

Several days passed before I found time to fulfil this request, and when I did go to Baker Street it was to find Mrs Hudson already informed of her lodger's impending arrival. The news, it seemed, had been brought by 'a gorgeous Dutchman'. From this I inferred that something else had indeed 'come up', but our landlady was unable to shed any further light on the matter. It was with a curious blend of sentiments that I climbed the seventeen steps to the rooms I had shared for so long. The grate was fireless, the air chilly and damp, but in my mind's eye I saw the coals blazing, and tea was on the table, and Holmes, his old dressing-gown wrapped about his tall spare figure, was explaining for my benefit the finer points of the case currently occupying his attention. Standing there in the dusk of a March afternoon, Sherlock Holmes seemed more of an enigma to me than ever. Who was he? That humane, pedantic figure whose spirit seemed even then to haunt the room? Or the soulless butcher in a fancy coat whose deeds had added another circle to the hell of Whitechapel? Which of these irreconcilable images was the true one? Would I ever know? But there was an even more urgent question demanding to be answered: who was Holmes now? Who was the man I would soon have to meet for the first time since we parted in Spitalfields that fateful night? The letters he had written seemed to augur well, but I could not accept them as conclusive proof that Holmes was cured. He had been driven to the murders, I believed, by a heady mixture of boredom and cocaine. As long as he remained abroad, amid novel sensations and fresh challenges, I had no fears for any relapse. But once he was ensconced again in the London he had himself described as a scene of 'familiar tedium', matters might quickly take a turn for the worse.

In the event, our reunion took place almost casually. I was returning home along Baker Street on the evening of the 20th of March, and glancing up at our rooms as I passed I was surprised to see the lamp lit, and on the blind a silhouette that was unmistakably that of my friend. I hastened to call, and was received with outward courtesy and perhaps some inward emotion. It transpired that he had only just arrived from Holland, where he had been detained for a few days by some business, details of which he declined to impart. I gathered that it had been a delicate matter involving the royal family of that country, but Holmes refused to be drawn on the subject. Of his other adventures, however, he spoke most readily, first of all relating the fascinating story behind the Trincomalee tragedy.

'I would not have missed it for the world,' he began, as we sat down before the fire in a manner pleasantly reminiscent of former times. 'Indeed, had I nothing else to show for my travels than that one case, I should consider my time well spent. Not that there was anything whatever of interest in either the motive or the method. The former was sordid and the latter commonplace. No, the whole interest of the affair turned on the way the criminals' best-laid schemes went very remarkably a-gley.'

'A what?'

' "A-gley." What, if we are to believe Burns, the schemes of mice and men—or in this case, a Mrs and her man—gang aft. The Mrs and Mrs Atkinson, Henry's wife, and her—'

'But how on earth can a man shoot another before a hundred witnesses and leave his body unmarked?' I cried impatiently.

'Good, Watson! With your customary unerring instinct you have singled out the one feature of this tangled puzzle which must be obvious to a child. There were no wounds on Henry's body for the excellent reason that there were no bullets in Edward's gun. The cartridges were blank.'

'Blank! But then why should—'

'But, you see, Edward did not know they were blank. He undoubtedly believed that he was going to shoot his brother. However, he also believed that when he did so, Henry would already be dead!'

'My dear Holmes!'

Having enjoined me not to interrupt, he went on to explain that the situation involved not two but three persons, the third being Henry's wife Elizabeth. The trio lived together in the Atkinson family mansion, a huge villa on the outskirts of Trincomalee. Henry was a domineering brute of a man, and violent and unpredictable in his cups. No doubt he was aware of the growing amity between his younger brother and his wife, who were almost of an age. As the daughter of a naval officer, Elizabeth had become accustomed to some degree of independence. Her husband treated her in the same style as he did his native workers. She for her part turned increasingly to Edward for friendship and protection, and a bond was formed between them which was strengthened equally by Henry's obnoxious presence and by his welcome and frequent absences on business. The outcome was inevitable. Henry returned unexpectedly one day to find Elizabeth and Edward in a situation which, though by no means immoral, clearly indicated that their relationship had passed beyond the purely legal, and was indeed hovering upon the brink of the impure and the illegal. Henry's response was typical of the man. He sent Elizabeth to her room, where he later used a horsewhip on her, and ordered Edward to be out of the house before sun-up.

'At this crisis, separate and alone, Elizabeth and Edward shared a common thought, a common dream of murder,' Holmes continued. 'But although their goal was the same, their plans for attaining it were characteristically different. Edward, with the straightforward impulsiveness of the male, decided to follow his brother around the plantations the next day and, at a suitable moment, to shoot him down. Elizabeth's feminine mind, on the other hand, turned to the subtler and more devious idea of poison. Moreover, she very astutely foresaw the course that would attract Edward, and since she could not put her plan into immediate effect, she decided to forestall him. At some time during that night she therefore contrived to unload Edward's revolver, replacing the live cartridges with blanks. She had now saved her lover from the gallows, as she saw it. At worst there would be another ugly scene between the brothers, and when night fell she would take care of Henry without putting either of them at risk.

'As it happened, Henry was accompanied all that day by a native overseer, and it was thus impossible for Edward to carry out the murderous attack he had planned.

Elizabeth, meanwhile, had not been idle. She had procured a quantity of a suitable alkaloid, which she meant to administer to her husband that evening at the Service Club where they went every Wednesday to play cards with a naval doctor and a captain. The doctor was notoriously gallant with the local belles, of whom Elizabeth Atkinson was a striking example. He was also rumoured to have lost a very considerable sum to Henry Atkinson at cards, by means the probity of which was open to question. In short, the doctor was a fine red herring to draw the police from Elizabeth's path. Let us not forget Edward, however. Having been foiled in the fields, he decided to stake out the house in hopes of shooting Henry as he entered or left. Again he was prevented, and was thus obliged to follow the couple down into Trincomalee. Whilst they and the naval officers settled down to their card game, Edward skulked about in the undergrowth, clutching a revolver which he had no idea was loaded only with blank cartridges. I cannot be certain exactly how much he guessed of Elizabeth's intentions. Certainly he was watching the foursome very closely. He may have noticed the wife mixing a powder into her husband's stengah. He must have seen the first spasm of agony cross Henry's brutal features. At that moment he thought only of Elizabeth, and of concealing her crime beneath his own. He therefore rushed into the club and emptied his harmless weapon into Henry's body. His brother crashed to the floor, his death throes being attributed to the action of the bullets. And thus ended a case which might aptly be entitled "The Tragedy of Errors".'

I shook my head in amazed admiration.

'Poetic justice, indeed!' I murmured. 'She sought to save her partner in sin, and in so doing hanged herself.'

Holmes laughed.

'Not unless she has done so since I sailed,' said he. 'But indeed, Mrs Elizabeth Atkinson did not impress me as a lady likely to fall prey to fits of excessive remorse.'

'But the trial—'

'Ah yes, the trial! Elizabeth was acquitted. Edward was found guilty of a breach of the peace and fined ten pounds.'

'But your case—'

'Oh, I know what happened, and I let them know that I knew, and I read in their eyes that I was right. But I could prove nothing. There was no evidence to connect Elizabeth with the poison that killed her husband, and without that my case was nothing but unsupported inference. For my part, I suspect her of coming to some arrangement with her medical admirer, whom she sought at the same time to incriminate! But no doubt you will rush to the defence of both your profession and the fair sex, and I must admit it is nothing but conjecture. My greatest problem was with the local people. They were solidly of the opinion that whoever had removed Henry Atkinson from their midst had performed a public service, and that interfering busybodies from England were distinctly unwelcome. I got the impression that if Mrs Elizabeth Atkinson chooses to remarry in a year or two without changing her name, the community will be perfectly willing to turn a blind eye. And who says crime does not pay!'

We continued to converse in this vein until a late hour. Holmes unravelled the complex web of political intrigue surrounding the Odessa murder, and recounted so many stirring and colourful episodes from his journey through the Caucasus and across the desert to Afghanistan that if I were to repeat but half of them here, my narrative would swell to a quite intolerable length. Our talk was both frank and free. We touched on every aspect of Holmes's adventures and of my new condition—save one. For in our midst, like the spectre at the banquet, walked the ghost of Professor Moriarty, whose name resounded still louder for being unspoken. In vain I waited for Holmes to mention the man who, not six months before, had obsessed his every waking moment. Finally, when we had begun to stifle yawns and to glance surreptitiously at the clock, I could restrain my curiosity no longer.

'But my dear Holmes, here it is almost midnight, and you still have not told me how you put paid to the infamous Moriarty!'

Holmes was gazing up at the mantelpiece as I spoke these words. I waited for his reply, but he sat quite silent, as if locked in position. His face went slack and bloodless, and his eyes seemed to stare with a hypnotic intensity. As the seconds ticked by in silence, I began to feel acutely embarrassed, as one must when so rational and self-possessed a man forgets himself. I was wondering how best I might cover for him, when the trance suddenly passed off.

'I do beg your pardon, Watson,' he said evenly. 'I was just following up a train of thought that occurred to me in connection with my last case. What was it you were saying?'

'I was enquiring about your final encounter with Professor Moriarty. Of course, I expect the Whitechapel horrors must seem like ancient history to you, but here in London they are still very much in the public mind What finally became of Jack the Ripper? In your telegram from Berne you said that he was dead, but how did it happen?'

My words came quickly and with a tremor I could not control, but Holmes seemed oblivious of my agitation.

'Yes, as you say, my experiences in the East have rather put that grisly business out of my head. But at all events, the public need trouble itself no longer about Moriarty. His tyranny is at an end.'

He would have left it at that, but I pressed him. Reluctantly he yielded up the information that the critical struggle had taken place in the Bernese Oberland, to which he had tracked the Professor across France and Germany.

'Finally Moriarty made a simple slip which enabled me to outmanœuvre him. He imagined he was deceiving me, while he was in fact playing into my hands. Our ultimate encounter took place at a famous falls, which I had already scouted as a suitable scene for my purpose.

On a narrow path cut into the rock of the abyss, we engaged in a final discussion of the questions which lay between us. His arguments proved the weaker.'

He spoke these words coldly and unwillingly. The contrast with his earlier sparkling bonhomie could not have been more marked. I was eager to hear how he would account for his actions after I had left him that night in Commercial Street, but to press him still further on a subject so obviously uncongenial, I realised, might well arouse his suspicions as to the reason for my excessive curiosity. That was the last thing I wanted. In fact, on mature consideration, I was inclined to think it no bad thing that Holmes sought to avoid the topic. It might well mean that he had determined to put that entire episode of his life into quarantine, as it were; to erase it from his memory as utterly as he claimed to have destroyed the man responsible.

We parted that night on the very best of terms, and within a few weeks I was once again regularly joining Holmes in his investigations into the cases which, as soon as news of his return became general, were once more brought in profusion to his door. A.C.D. included accounts of most of these adventures in the stories he published after Holmes's death, so I will content myself with merely naming them. Following the Irene Adler affair in March, we investigated the events culminating in the robbery at Mawson & Williams's, and later in June the strange disappearance of Neville St Clair. July was a busy month, providing us with three cases—that of my old school friend 'Tadpole' Phelps and the missing treaty; that which bore on the loss of the barque *Sophy Anderson*; and the highly sensitive affair arising from a duel fought in Windsor Great Park. In August, my records reveal, we were able to exonerate Mrs Nancy Barclay of her husband's murder, while September found us solving the riddles of Miss Mary Sutherland's absconding fiancé, Mr Hatherley's missing thumb, and Mr Openshaw's orange pips. In November, Holmes was able to foil an ingenious attempt to steal the Rosetta Stone, and the year ended with our unex-

pected recovery of the Countess of Morcar's diamond.*
This list will in itself demonstrate that throughout 1889
I kept very close watch on Sherlock Holmes. My practice, which had never been large, shrank almost to nothing as a result of my continual preoccupation with the
doings of my friend, and I fear that my wife must on
occasion have been sorely tried by my apparent irre-
sponsibility. But I was rewarded, come the new year, by
my confident conviction that all was well with Holmes,
and that whatever fit had temporarily eclipsed his genius
in the autumn of '88 had passed away without leaving
any traces. As of old, he seemed happy to turn his attention to any problem that might be laid before him,
and the cases we investigated together represent only a
fraction of those tackled by him that year. In short,
Holmes resembled no one so much as the vigorous and
enthusiastic man I had met in 1881. The transformation
was so complete that it was with relief rather than surprise that I found myself, one day in September, being
presented with the bottle of cocaine solution and the little morocco case that contained his needles.

'Perhaps you may be able to find some use for these,
Doctor,' he declared. 'For my part, I no longer need
them. The supply of work has been quite adequate thus
far, but if it fails I shall resort to certain respiratory
techniques which I mastered during my stay in the East.
The effect is quite as satisfactory, and there are no sec-
ondary complications.'

I took the instruments of evil from his hand with unfeigned satisfaction. This was indeed something! If he
had come to understand the danger cocaine represented
to his welfare, and was determined to renounce it, then
surely he was well on his way to a complete recovery.

Before leaving these months when Sherlock Holmes
was, all unwittingly, on probation, I must record one
incident which caused me much concern at the time and

---

*All but three of these cases appear among Conan Doyle's
stories. The exceptions are the case assigned to November,
and the last two of the three cases assigned to July. For further details of the July cases, see note to p. 136.

was to have a profound effect on later events. One Wednesday morning in mid-July a woman named Alice McKenzie was found in an alley off Whitechapel High Street, her throat cut and her abdomen ripped open. I read about the crime in that day's *Telegraph,* which commented that the murder was certainly one of the series which had startled London the previous winter. Later editions were even more positive. All were agreed that the atrocity was the work of Jack the Ripper.

I felt as though I had been hit by a shell. All the comforting certainties with which I had been busily surrounding myself hung in tattered shreds. Then hope returned, as I recalled that Holmes had not been alone on the night in question. On the contrary, he had been at home in the company of myself and two of Europe's most distinguished criminal investigators—Monsieur Dubuque and Herr von Waldbaum. The occasion had been a dinner to mark the successful conclusion of the case I have mentioned arising from a duel fought at Windsor. This affair, which involved members of three royal families in situations of an extremely compromising nature, had best remain undisclosed even now. I will refer to it as the case of the second slain. Those who are familiar with the events in question will instantly apprehend my meaning.* The investigation, involving as it did the interests of so many highly placed persons, had been conducted jointly by Holmes and the two foreign agents I have named. These gentlemen had taken a markedly different view of the case from Holmes's, but a mutual respect prevailed throughout and when

---

*This case is not among those treated by Conan Doyle. However, in 'The Naval Treaty' we find this passage: 'The July which immediately succeeded my marriage was made memorable by three cases . . . I find them recorded in my notes under the headings of "The Adventure of the Second Stain", "The Adventure of the Naval Treaty", and "The Adventure of the Tired Captain."' If we identify the final pair with the first two of Watson's cases for July 1889 (see p. 135) then by a process of elimination Watson's 'case of the second slain' and Conan Doyle's 'Adventure of the Second Stain' must be one and the same.

Holmes proved to have been correct his first wish was to discuss his methods and findings with his rivals. Thus it was that the great symposium was convened. I was privileged to be present, and still retain an almost verbatim account of the proceedings.

Never will I forget that evening! Much of what was said passed my understanding at the time, but one could sense the air fairly crackling under the communicated energies of those three finely attuned minds. For each it was a unique opportunity to exchange the ideas that were the very breath of their lives with men fully capable of comprehending them. For once, Holmes found himself free of the need to make allowances for his audience, and the result was a discussion of such ferocious brilliance as I never expect to hear again.

On the face of it, one could hardly wish for a better alibi. But was it an alibi? I myself had been obliged to leave the gathering shortly before eleven o'clock. By then the case of the second slain had been thoroughly talked out, but the conversation had gravitated towards the more general aspects of investigative work and was still going strong when I left. Since McKenzie had been murdered some time between midnight and one o'clock, the point I had urgently to clarify was how long the two Continental detectives had remained with Holmes.

Monsieur Dubuque had already returned to Paris, but I was fortunate enough to catch Herr von Waldbaum at his hotel. I invented some clumsy story about wishing to know if my brother had called in search of me at about midnight. The German replied that he was unable to enlighten me, having himself left Holmes's rooms before that hour. Dubuque, however, had remained and might be able to assist me—although a simpler course, *natürlich*, would be to ask Herr Holmes himself. Alas, I muttered, that was not possible. A question of family honour was involved. Von Waldbaum nodded gravely.

I left the hotel in an agony of suspense. For a moment I thought of cabling Dubuque, but I soon realised that the matter was too delicate to be adequately conveyed in telegraphic jargon. Above all, I had to drop some hint, as I had with the German, that would prevent Dubuque telling Holmes about my inquisitiveness. There is only one way to be sure that a hint has been taken—especially across a language barrier—and that is by reading your man's eyes. I therefore hurried home, packed a few necessities, told my wife an untruth, and caught the night express to Paris. The following morning I had a brief interview with Monsieur Dubuque at the Sûreteé. With the Frenchman I thought it best to amend my tale. After a lengthy exchange of compliments I asked him, in a suitably halting fashion, whether Holmes had received an unexpected visit from a lady between twelve and one on the night in question. Dubuque was highly taken with the idea of the great English detective and celebrated misogynist being entangled in such an affair, but was able to assure me that he and Holmes had continued to *bavarder* until after one o'clock, and that no such clandestine rendezvous had been attempted during that time. But then a man of sense and discretion such as Monsieur Holmes would without doubt have arranged some signal to his *belle inconnue*. I agreed that this might well be the case, but my relief on learning that Holmes had not done the murder and that all was still well was so evidently unfeigned that Dubuque immediately assumed that some rivalry existed between Holmes and myself for the attentions of the lady in question! I entreated him to say nothing of this to Holmes; he seemed offended that I felt it necessary to ask. He quoted La Rochefoucauld; I resisted the temptation to embrace him in the Latin manner, took my leave, rushed into the first café I saw and consumed a pint of champagne.

Whether it was the wine or the good news, I unfortunately omitted to remove the labels from my luggage on my return to London that evening. Mary was at first reluctant to accept my explanation for the presence of a tab reading 'Paris via Dover' on a bag which had supposedly accompanied me to Midhurst in Sussex, where I had supposedly been assisting Holmes to solve the mystery of the corpse on the beach. She protested, among other things, that there was no beach at Midhurst. That, I replied darkly, was the mystery. So ended the episode of the first return of Jack the Ripper, which began with high drama, seemed set to turn to tragedy, and ended perilously close to farce. I came out of it more than ever convinced—with that irrational complacency which is the natural result of a false alarm—that Holmes could now be trusted to his own devices.

My Paddington practice, meanwhile, was doomed. The rot caused by my constant attendance on Holmes was too far gone to be eradicated, and the resulting air of gloom and failure which hung over my consulting-room proved to be an effective deterrent to new patients. After some deliberation I therefore decided to sell out and move to another district, where I might start afresh. It seemed an auspicious moment for such a change. The new decade promised a fresh start for me too. I had fulfilled my duty to society. The Whitechapel murders had evidently come to an end, and Holmes was no longer a danger to the public. The time had come to consider myself for a change. At the end of January 1890 I found a suitable practice in Kensington. Now at last I could begin my married life in earnest, unencumbered by responsibilities left over from my bachelorhood. A new era seemed to beckon me, and a new life as a family man and a successful physician with a flourishing practice in a fashionable area suitably distant from Baker Street. No longer could I be at Holmes's beck and call. From now onwards my patients and my household must claim prior importance.

The financial strain imposed by the move was considerable. My Paddington practice I disposed of for rather more than it was perhaps worth, but my wife was nevertheless compelled to sell another of the fabulous pearls she had received as conscience money from Mr Thaddeus Sholto. Indeed, the Sholto case helped us in more than one way, for it formed the basis of A.C.D.'s second story based on Holmes's work, which was written at this time. I was a little surprised to find him reverting to a form with which he had seemingly finished for ever, but apparently 'A Study in Scarlet' had enjoyed a success in America, and an American magazine had now commissioned him to provide a sequel. The arrangement A.C.D. sought was as before. I was to provide the raw material from my notes and personal reminiscences, while he would give the thing form and style. I was obliged to consult Holmes of course, and remembering his outburst on reading A.C.D.'s treatment of the Jefferson Hope case, I did so with some trepidation. But to my great surprise, Holmes gave his consent at once. He seemed mildly amused that the Americans had so relished 'A Study in Scarlet'. But which case was my friend preparing to trivialise now? I suggested that perhaps the Sholto affair might prove suitable for fictional treatment.

'Ah yes!' Holmes smiled fondly. 'Mr Thaddeus and Brother Bartholomew! Jonathan Small and Tonga!'

'And Mary Morstan.'

'Quite. Yes, I have no doubt it has all the ingredients of a successful novelette. Needless to say, I do not expect your colleague to capture anything but the crude outlines of my method. But hopefully the affair already possesses enough romance and pathos to satisfy his readership, thus sparing him the necessity of interpolating frontier melodramas of his own invention.'

When 'The Sign of Four; or, The Problem of the Sholtos' duly appeared in February, I had not seen Holmes for over six weeks. So effective was my determination to change my ways, indeed, that throughout 1890 we met only four, possibly five, times. Only twice did I accompany him on an investigation, as against a dozen such instances the previous year. In June we travelled to Herefordshire to look into the murder of Charles McCarthy, and in October I was at his side when he foiled the Saxe-Coburg Square bank raid.* No doubt I was at fault in washing my hands of Holmes in

*For further details of these cases, see 'The Boscombe Valley Mystery' and 'The Red-Headed League', respectively.

this cavalier fashion. No doubt I should have withdrawn more gradually, and returned more often to check that all was well. But in all honesty, I am afraid that if I had noticed any signs of mischief at 221B Baker Street I would simply have looked the other way. Having braved such a monster, and seen it dead and buried, it is hard to admit that the ground above its grave is cracked and heaving.

However, the question did not arise. I was aware of no change in Holmes. Indeed, I had virtually ceased to be aware of Holmes at all. My life seemed sunny and serene as never before. Christmas came and went, and it was 1891. I was a respected physician with a growing practice and the contented master of a well-ordered household. Jack the Ripper seemed already a thing of the past, locked away between the pages of yellowing newspapers like all the dead who once strutted so boldly. But Jack was not dead. He was only resting, and his rest had almost reached its term.

## Five

Frances Coles, a Whitechapel prostitute of the lowest type, was murdered shortly after two o'clock in the morning of Friday the 13th February 1891. Her body was found by a patrolling policeman in an alley under one of the arches of the railway bridge between Chamber Street and Royal Mint Street. Her throat had been horridly cut. The evening papers carried several columns on the subject, and none professed the slightest doubt that the killing was the work of Jack the Ripper. The police were strongly censured for having relaxed their vigilance; the public warned to brace itself for a fresh onslaught of terror.

I read the reports with a wry smile and a pleasant sense of superiority. It was perfectly clear to me that the murder had no connection whatever with the earlier series. I knew who had been responsible for those atrocities, and after making myself ridiculous over the last Ripper scare, I had no intention of being drawn every time a Whitechapel whore had her throat cut and the press, knowing it was worth an extra hundred thousand copies, attributed the crime to Jack the Ripper. Within a few days a seaman was arrested for the murder, and although he was subsequently acquitted, I gathered that the authorities were convinced that he had in fact killed not only Coles but Alice McKenzie as well.

At about this time Holmes left for the Continent, having apparently been engaged by the French Government in a matter of supreme importance. I received two letters from him. The first was a mere conventional note, remarkable only because Holmes was not in the habit of writing conventional notes. The second letter, in contrast, was of so singular a character that I had better reproduce it here exactly as I received it:

Nîmes
April 1st

Dear Watson,

I am sure you cannot have forgotten Miss Gloria Scott, of whom I told you so much in connection with the Trevors of Donnithorpe? You will no doubt be enlightened to know that she is now staying here, acting as interpreter to poor English folk in distress. We met only last evening, when she told me about 'the eminent scientist, Professor Nemo. He is apparently still alive. I understood he had been killed while developing France's industrial resources (coals, iron, etc.) I myself, essentially, am now engaged on carrying further his researches. His trail remains clear. My old tutor's post at Montpellier is vacant—a watched pot, perhaps, cannot boil. You say: "Tell me more, Holmes!" But this isn't the time. Remember what he wrote—"Truth shall run, but not hide, nor escape secretly from me." ' Poor English, indeed, but excellent sense.

Yours<br>Holmes

I was greatly alarmed by the disordered state of mind revealed by this letter. A ship named *Gloria Scott* had indeed figured in one of Holmes's early cases, which he had related to me, but no such lady. As for Professor Nemo, not only had I never heard of him, I very much doubted whether any such person existed outside the pages of fiction. But what I found most disturbing was the disintegration of Holmes's normally immaculate style the relative coherence of the first lines to the halting gibberish of the last. All in all, the letter reminded me horribly of the scribbles of a drug maniac.

About three weeks after I received this queer communication, I was sitting up late one evening in my consulting-room. My wife was staying with her aunt. I was poring over the latest issues of the medical press when suddenly the door swung open and on the threshold there appeared a gaunt apparition that I recognised, after a few moments, as Sherlock Holmes. I was still staring dumbly in shock when he dropped to his hands and knees and scuttled at great speed across the floor to the window. Reaching up, he pulled the shutters together and bolted them.

'Holmes!' I cried. 'What has happened? You look terrible!'

In truth I had never before seen my old friend so pale and haggard. His features were drawn and lined, so that he appeared prematurely aged, while the trembling of his limbs spoke eloquently of his exhaustion. He edged around my desk, inspecting the room warily. At last he dropped into a chair, shading his eyes from my lamp.

'What is it, Holmes? Are you afraid of something?'

'Of someone.'

'But of whom?'

He squinted blearily at me.

'Did you not get my letter? Was it intercepted, then?'

I stared at him fixedly.

'Your letter?'

'From Nîmes.'

'Certainly I got it. But I fear I have no recollection of any of the persons you named. Is it they who are pursuing you?'

Holmes sighed. He drew a cigarette from his case, studied it for a moment, and then glanced up at me.

'I see. No doubt I expected too much. Might I trouble you for a match? I must apologise for calling so late. A few pence will see the pantry window mended, and then I should have it barred before one of the light-fingered gentry avails himself of the same facility. Is Mrs Watson in?'

'My wife is away on a visit.'

'Indeed? You are alone, then? Yes, of course—the hatstand. You must forgive my obtusity. I have not slept more than a few minutes these fourteen days. I cannot rest. He will gain the upper hand if I rest. But I grow slow, Watson, and that too may be fatal.'

'Look, Holmes, I don't know what you are talking about, but I know a case of utter exhaustion when I see one. You cannot continue to expend your strength without allowing the organism to recuperate. Your will may carry you further than other men, but you are still human. You must sleep here tonight. We shall be alone, and I will stay up to see that no harm befalls you.'

Holmes shook his head sadly.

'Your offer is most generous, Watson, but I must refuse. If you knew the nature of the threat I represent, you would not be so free with your hospitality. I am cursed, Watson! The house in which I lay my head is visited by evil in the night. But if you would help me tomorrow. Would you be willing to accompany me to the Continent for a few days?'

'To the Continent? But where are you going?'

He waved vaguely.

'Going? I am not going anywhere. I am fleeing, Watson—fleeing for my life! We must go where he will not find us. Ha! He will find us wherever we go!'

I strained forward.

'But of whom are you speaking, Holmes?'

He started.

'Eh? Why, Professor Moriarty, of course!'

'What? But Moriarty is dead!'

'Dead, is he?' screamed Holmes in a fit of fury. 'Oh, very well! Whatever you like! Of course, it may prove necessary to redefine what you mean by dead, if the term is to be applied to people who can fire air-guns, wield knives, murder unfortunates, and drive the foremost criminal agent in Europe to the brink of nervous exhaustion!'

I was by now confused beyond measure.

'But Holmes, you told me he was dead, did you not?'

'I told you that I had been mistaken, that he had survived and was once more at large.'

'You told me that? But when? Where?'

'In my letter, man! In a cipher so elementary I thought even you might be able to fathom it. The *Gloria Scott* case, Watson! Every third word! Oh, no matter. The fact is that Moriarty has returned from the dead and is loose in the streets of London. It was he who killed that woman Coles, and he would have had more since then had I not prevented him. Again and again he strove to break away, but as often I headed him off. I tell you, my friend, that if a detailed account of these eight weeks past could be written, it would count as the most brilliant piece of thrust-and-parry work in the history of detection. It has left both of us desperate and exhausted men. There is no holding back now, no sense of fair play. There is only the instinct to destroy meeting its implacable opposite, and the first of us to give an inch is a dead man. It is him or me, Watson, by fair means or foul!'

For a long moment he was silent, his head resting wearily in his cupped hands. Then he roused himself once more, and looked up at me imploringly.

'That is why I am here. God knows I have no wish to bring danger to your house, but I am left with no alternative. I need your help, Watson, and I need it desperately! Moriarty and I are so finely matched that it is an impasse between us. Your help, perhaps, will swing the matter in my favour. A week, Watson! No more than a week. Will you come? It will be like old times. Say you will come!'

There were tears in my eyes, and in my breast an indescribable conflict of emotions, as I fervently replied:

'Old fellow, can you doubt it?'

He smiled, and lay back in the chair. A few minutes later his eyes were closed, the cigarette had dropped cold from his fingers, and he was asleep. I went to my dispensary and made up a mildly soporific solution, which I injected into Holmes's forearm. My first thought was to ensure that his rest was unbroken. With the assistance of my cook—a muscular Irishwoman—I moved the unconscious Holmes upstairs, and laid him down on a bed in the spare room. Having seen that he was comfortable, I locked the door on the outside and returned downstairs. I then poured myself a large whisky, and tried to think what the devil I was to do.

I was under no illusions as to the gravity of the situation. The cipher in Holmes's letter might have got by me, but his conversational code I could now read with ease. I knew whom he meant in naming Moriarty, and I understood perfectly the nature of the struggle taking place between himself and the Professor. If Holmes was mad, it was, as one might have expected, a methodical madness. His great mind was in ruins, but in those ruins life went on. Did he know what he had done? In some remaining enclave of sanity, was he aware of what he had become? So it seemed, and finding the madness too powerful to master, he had grappled with it in the darkness of his soul and thrown it out, and called it Moriarty. Everything he did and said had to be not merely observed but interpreted, as one interprets a charade. His words, which seemed a wild nightmare if literally understood, made only too clear a sense once one grasped that everything of which he spoke was taking place within the confines of his own brain.

No doubt in my heart I had always known that this moment must arrive. How else could I have found myself so clear-headed, so unamazed—so relieved almost—now that the storm had finally broken? It had been a close and sultry interlude, full of wishful thinking and cowardly self-deception. I had known all the time what had to be done. All my doubts and my evasions were only attempts to deny that grim knowledge. I had known that such things as I had witnessed in Miller's Court do not heal themselves with fresh air and exercise. They have to be destroyed. I had known that since the 9th of November 1888, but how I had hoped it might not prove necessary. How I had hoped I might be spared! And now another woman lay murdered, and her blood was on my head as surely as if I had struck her down myself. I found my conduct thus far utterly contemptible, and I turned from it in disgust. I could not mend it, but I could at least put an end to my vacillation and act the man for once.

I trust that the reader, having patiently followed me so far, will not now give me up for lost when I confess that even at this eleventh hour I could not wholly convince myself of Holmes's guilt. If I were one of our psychological novelists I could perhaps hope to convey the subtle shadings of reservation and misgiving which mottled the almost solid certainty of my mind. As it is, I can only say that, for all I had, I needed yet one more piece of evidence; some final spark to ignite the mass of material I had laboriously gathered. For a time was coming when I must confront Holmes, look him in the eyes and tell him what I knew. Such was the man's mastery over me of old, I was terribly afraid that at the last

I might funk it. If I were to free myself for ever of his influence, I needed some final irrefutable proof of what he had become, so that I could go forth with furious dispassion and do what had to be done.

I fetched my coat and hat, looked in on Holmes, who remained in a deep sleep, and then left the house. In the High Street I found a cab, which set me down some fifteen minutes later outside 221 Baker Street. I had removed Holmes's keychain before leaving, and a minute later I was standing in the familiar front room. Nothing seemed to have changed, except that the disorder was even more marked than I remembered it. The floor was virtually impassable for mounds of newspaper. Drawers hung open and overflowing, and every horizontal surface supported an assortment of objects in fantastic juxtaposition. I stood for a full five minutes, gazing at this scene with a sinking heart, and then I took off my coat and set to work. It took me almost four hours to complete my search, but by then I had turned out and sifted through every article in those rooms, and I had found nothing one might not reasonably expect to find in the chambers of a gentleman of eccentric tastes. I certainly had not found that final damning proof I longed for— and dreaded. I collapsed despondently in Holmes's velvet-lined chair and lit a cigarette. It was four o'clock in the morning. In a few hours Holmes would wake. Then what? Could I let him go, knowing what I did? Could I do otherwise, knowing no more? Unconscious I had risen from my chair and started to pace the floor, as Holmes would when his mind was working on a problem. At length, tiring of picking a path through the piles of newsprint, I stopped in front of the tall windows and stared out at the bleak canyon of Baker Street, and up at the dark sky where all too soon the first shimmer of dawn would appear.

The truth struck me all at once. One moment I stood gazing aimlessly out of the window, the next I was rummaging furiously through the contents of Holmes's desk. I soon found the small leather case I was looking for. With it concealed under my coat I quietly left the house, walked up to the corner, and turned into Blandford Street. I looked around to ensure that I was not observed before slipping into the mews. I passed the first house and stopped by the wooden gate giving into the yard of the second. It was unlocked. I passed through. The windows of the property were dark and curtainless. The back door was locked. I got out the case, which contained Holmes's house-breaking tools. I had studied my friend's methods on several occasions when he had deemed it necessary to enter a building without the consent of the owner, and although the finer points of the art were lost on me I could force a door as well as any man. In a minute I was standing in a bare passage, whose peeling paper and damp odour told of a long period of disuse and neglect. I lit the dark lantern which was another feature of the burglary kit, and began my search.

The house was in every respect the opposite of Number 221, which it faced across Baker Street. This even extended to the condition of the rooms, which—save one—were all bare and empty. The sole exception was the first-floor bedroom, at the rear of the premises. This was fully but simply furnished: a bed, a wardrobe, a wash-stand, a chest of drawers. Like Holmes's room at 221B, to which it corresponded, it also contained a tin chest filled with papers and mementoes. The papers were of two sorts. First, there were cuttings from the press reports of the Whitechapel murders. These were stuffed into cardboard boxes. The texts were heavily underscored in parts, and sprinkled with marginal comments and exclamation marks. There were also several bundles of handwritten papers in the chest, tied up neatly with red tape. At first sight these looked exactly like the records of past cases which Holmes kept in the chest in his room. But these were records of a very different kind: exhaustive, graphic, gloating accounts of each of the Whitechapel murders, written by the murderer. I burned the papers later, for they were not fit to be read, but I kept back one sheet which will serve to give the flavour of the collection. It was a sort of index,

written in the bold coarse hand whose letters had popu-
larised the name of Jack the Ripper, and it ran as follows:

### Curriculum Mortis

Hors d'oeuvre—Martha Tabram. A saucy little stab-
bing in the George Yard Buildings    dont go away it
gets better

7 August 88
1 Mary Ann Nicholls—the first work to show the
power of the masters hand SLASHING CLEAN THREW
HER BLOOMIN THROTE now Jack's work is done the
pubs lost its pun*

August 31st
2 Annie Chapman (she told me Sivvey)—a highly
polished performance—polished her off ha ha!
Sliced her very nicely from her hot spot to her dugs
8th of September 1888 R.I.P. ha ha
A double treat!
3 Elizabeth Stride. Just had the big bitch pinned
when the Philistine Jew has to come by and ruin all
the beauty of it    ah but

4 Catherine Eddowes—soaring free above the foul
unfettered finding killing and utterly gutting the pig-
bag motherscum RIPRIPRIPRIPRIPRIPRIPRIPRIPRIPRIP
RIP
And that's the long and the short of it
say old Boss did you ever think it Mitre been them
Masons?
The thirtieth of September in this fear of our bawds
1888

---

*The pub in question is probably The Roebuck, which still
stands at the corner of Brady Street and Durward Street. The
pun arose from the fact that Durward Street was originally
called Buck's Row; it was lost when the name was changed
following a petition by the residents after Mary Ann Nicholls
was murdered.

5 Mary Jane Kelly
Look on my works, ye Mighty, and despair!

9 November     lady marys day

op. post. Frances Coles.
Old mother Coles
Was the first of the souls
To be chived since he rose from the dead
Her throat's cut so fine
You can tickle her spine
And play skittle-ball with her head
13 February 1891    unlucky for some


At the bottom of the chest, when I had removed all
the papers, I found a small wooden box and three glass
vessels. The box contained a quantity of cheap jewel-
lery, several locks of hair, a scrap of cloth, part of a
broken mirror, a candle stub, two farthings, some
matches, and a human tooth. The glass vessels were of
the kind used in hospitals to retain organs for examination. They were filled with a colourless fluid, and wax-
sealed. The first two I looked at held various abdominal
organs. Amongst the contents I recognised part of a
liver, a section of duodenum, a kidney, and a short
length of urethra. The last jar—
(I broke off here, hoping I might omit this final obscene detail. But I am pursuaded that without it my
subsequent behaviour may not be fully understood.)
The last jar contained portions of a uterus, together
with a foetus of some twelve or fourteen weeks' growth.
A paper label bearing six lines of writing was pasted to
the glass.

> Once in royal Victoria's city
> stood a lowly courtyard shed
> Where a Mother took a stranger
> He took her, and now she's dead:
> Kelly was that Mother wild
> In this jar her little child.

It would be no undue exaggeration to say that those six lines sealed Holmes's fate. I had asked for some proof so gross and blatant that our friendship would be dissolved as if in acid, leaving me free to destroy a stranger and a murderer. Here was my proof, and its effect was everything I had asked for—and more. Strictly speaking I could have washed my hands of the business there and then. I had only to call Lestrade and show him what I had found, and then to take him to my house and give Holmes over into his keeping. But it was too late for such half-measures. If I had discovered just the papers and the jars, without that jeering verse, I might have been content to play Judas. But I was personally involved now. The abomination Holmes had become threatened everything I hold dear and by which I have lived my life. The last thing I wished was to see such filth besmirch for ever the image of a man whom others besides myself had come to regard as among the best and the wisest England had produced. It would have been a terrible and damaging blow to the moral fibre of the entire nation if Sherlock Holmes had been identified in open court as the author of those lines. My legal duty gave way before a sense of obligation to my country and to the great deal of enlightened rationalism which Holmes himself personified. If the events of the next ten days revealed a Watson whose existence no one—least of all myself—had previously suspected, the cause may be traced directly to that scrap of demonic doggerel.

I let myself out of that house, which Holmes had pointed out to me long before as Moriarty's lair, shortly before five o'clock. I felt strangely calm and deliberate, but also elated. The morning air seemed to have been wafted straight from some mountain peak. I inhaled it gratefully as the cab jingled me home through the awakening city. How singular, I thought, that dull stolid uninspiring John Watson should have been selected as the instrument of fate!

My first task on returning home was to replace Holmes's keys. He was still sleeping, and I took the opportunity to search his clothes for weapons and drugs. I found neither. His only possessions, besides the keychain, were a little money, his cigarettes, a ham sandwich wrapped in paper, and a small horn snuffbox. Having satisfied myself on this point, I relocked the bedroom door and made my way downstairs, where I wrote two letters. The first was a short personal note to my wife, containing as much of the truth as I thought she should know. The other was a detailed communication addressed to Inspector Lestrade. Although I was determined to settle the account with Holmes myself, I was not foolhardy enough to assume I would necessarily be successful. My own life I was prepared to hazard, but I could not permit Holmes to go free if I failed. I therefore told Lestrade what had happened, and what I had found, and what I was attempting, and hinted broadly that if I were to die as the result of an accident in the next few weeks, the circumstances might well bear looking into. This letter I sealed in an envelope addressed to my bank manager, instructing him to forward the contents on the 8th of May. When the maid appeared to lay the fire, I gave her the letter with instructions to put it in the post that morning without fail. I then sent her off to pack some necessities in a small case.

By now my sleeplessness was beginning to take its toll, and as I considered the prospect before me it became clear that this was going to be a continuing problem. The scene Holmes had painted for me the night before, of two exhausted men each willing himself to stay alert longer than the other, now took on a more immediate significance. Obviously I could not leave Holmes unwatched for even a few minutes. There was quite literally no telling what he might do, and even if it were nothing more than a decampment in flight from imaginary enemies, it would mean the end of all my hopes for a decent solution to this horribly indecent business. Evidently if I was to retain the advantage I had to have some artificial support denied to Holmes. I had made sure that he was without needles or bottles, but what was I to do? I had nothing suitable to hand, and by the time the chemists' shops opened Holmes would be up and about. Then, suddenly, I remembered the gift which Holmes had made to me of his hypodermic needles and his cocaine solution. Cocaine was by no means ideal for my purposes, but its action is stimulating to the central nervous system and if used judiciously I had no doubt it would fit the bill. I located the small brown bottle in one of the drawers of my desk, transferred the contents to a larger container marked 'The Linctus', and diluted them considerably. I then injected a small amount into my arm. The effect was immediate and remarkable. I felt my head clear, my spirits lift, my limbs surge with energy. Yes, it would do! I set the bottle and the case of needles on one side, and went upstairs to see how my guest was faring.

As I opened the door I noticed at once that the bed was now empty. In the same instant Holmes leapt out from behind the door and swung at my head with a fireiron. Only the hypersensitive reactions which are a product of the drug saved my life. I sensed the attack just in time, and the weapon caught me only a glancing blow. This was still enough to stun me momentarily. I came to lying on the floor with Holmes bent over me. His arms were around me and his face was filled with anxiety.

'You're not hurt, Watson?' he cried. 'For God's sake, say that you are not hurt!'

I rose groggily to my feet.

'It's nothing.'

'Ah, the fiend! You see how cunning he is! He makes me almost kill my only friend! He knew that after seeing his man in the garden I would assume that he had done away with you, and was coming to finish me off.'

'In the garden? His man?'

He plucked me by the sleeve and led me over to the window.

'No, stand back! Like so, at the side. Do you see him?'

'William? He comes every Saturday, to do the garden.'

'Ha! Clearly Moriarty foresaw the utility of having an agent with access to your household. Your domestics may also have been suborned. I should never have stayed here, Watson. It was madness. We have been very fortunate thus far, but the Professor may strike at any moment. We must leave at once. Every second is precious.'

'My luggage is packed.'

Holmes gave out an exclamation of disgust.

'No luggage, man! You might as well tell him which station we are headed for and save him any further trouble in the matter. We will go as we are, and encourage the manufactures of the countries through which we travel. But first we must think of a *beau stratagème* to get out of this house alive.'

Whilst Holmes paced the floor, wrestling with this imaginary problem, I was trying to answer the rather more vital question of how to take along the cocaine and syringe unobserved, since we were to travel without luggage. The thought of the drug gave me an idea.

'I say, Holmes! How would it be if I got myself up as if I were paying a visit to a patient? You know—morning-dress and black bag. Surely he would not suspect that?'

Holmes gave me an approving glance.

'Excellent, Watson! I see that you are in form today. I had the same idea two minutes ago. What was giving me pause was the question of how my own exit might be managed. Now I have that too.'

He would say no more, but bade me go and change. When the maid called me, I was to go straight down and get into the waiting cab. Evidently Holmes was indulging himself in that strain of arch mystification I had come to know so well. It seemed best to humour him, so I went to my room to don my professional attire. I had scarcely finished packing my medical bag—it was rather weightier than usual, what with the cocaine, the case of needles, a purse of gold coins, and my service revolver—when the maid knocked to tell me that my cab was at the door. I hastened downstairs. A hansom was drawn up at the kerb. I climbed in without a word and the driver promptly whipped up his horse. We drove smartly through the residential streets of the district and turned out into Cromwell Road. Our pace here was such that we were soon overtaking all other traffic. Passing the great façade of the new museum, we drew level with an unoccupied four-wheeler. I heard my cabbie hail his opposite number.

'You free, mate?' he cried. 'There's a growler wanted in Alfred Place West.* Down by the railway station. I just come from there!'

The other waved acknowledgment and turned off to the right. At the next corner we followed suit. We sped furiously down the street, rounded the corner on one wheel, raced to the end, and drew in at the Metropolitan station. My driver leapt down from his perch and secured the reins to a lamp-standard.

'Come, Watson! There's not a moment to lose!' cried Sherlock Holmes.

A few words with the maid had in fact prepared me for this revelation, but any want of warmth in my response went unnoticed as Holmes led me at a run into the station. Instead of turning down the steps leading to the trains, however, he continued at full stride the length of the short arcade. Dashing out the other side, he crossed the road and climbed into the four-wheeler that was just drawing up. I scrambled in after him, Holmes rapped loudly on the roof, and in another moment we were mobile again.

'Might I trouble you for a cigar, Doctor?' asked Holmes with a twinkle. 'All this fresh air calls for a chaser.'

Now I had to hear how he had told Jane to run to the High Street cab rank and summon the tallest and thinnest driver to my address, where he was induced by

---

*Now Thurloe Street. The 'new museum' Watson refers to is evidently the Natural History Museum, completed in 1880.

means of a sum of money to exchange clothes with Holmes and to part with his cab for half an hour, at the end of which time he was to take a train to the South Kensington station and retrieve it. Moriarty would of course assume, on seeing us enter the station, that we had resorted to the railway, into whose nether depths he would descend whilst we sped away unpursued, etc., etc. Dutifully I gasped and nodded and exclaimed. What did it matter? Let Holmes amuse himself. He might elude Moriarty, but he could not escape me.

There were still two hours to wait before the departure of the boat train. We occupied this time with a long drive across the river to Peckham, where we breakfasted amply in an establishment frequented almost exclusively by omnibus drivers. Shortly before eleven o'clock we drew up in the concourse at Victoria Station. I remained in the cab while Holmes purchased the tickets. At his signal I joined him, and we both then rushed headlong through the milling throng and clambered aboard the already moving train. Needless to say this behaviour, together with the eccentricity of our apparel, attracted some little attention. But it was not this which caused Holmes to utter an oath as he gazed back at the receding platform.

'Damn! It's Moriarty!'

I rushed to see, but another train pulling out hid the station from view. Holmes smote the partition of our compartment in frustration and anger.

'The cunning devil! He must have gambled that we were heading for the Continent. When we gave him the slip he simply made for Victoria and sat down to wait. It is what I myself would have done in the circumstances. It is well we took no chances at the station! But I fear we are up against it once more, friend Watson.'

By now this continued pantomime was beginning to pall on me, and I found it hard to keep my voice from betraying that fact.

'I scarcely see what good it can do him to know we have caught this train. It is an express, and the boat runs in connection with it. Even if he engages a special he must arrive too late.'

Holmes favoured me with a pitying smile.

'My dear Watson, you evidently did not realize my meaning when I said that this man may be taken as being quite on the same intellectual plane as myself. His plans have been laid for months, and you can be certain that he will not have overlooked the possibility of my escaping him in London. Our train may achieve sixty miles an hour, but the impulses in those wires'—he pointed out of the window—'travel at the speed of thought. Even if we break every record for the run, Moriarty's henchmen in Dover will have well over an hour to prepare for our arrival, and when we step from this carriage we will be as good as dead!'

'If that is the case,' I muttered, 'we had better say our prayers. The train does not stop, and there is no way out of this compartment.'

Holmes took a large pinch of snuff and settled back in the corner without a word. The train sped on, shaking off the tentacles of suburban London and striking out into the vernal Kentish countryside. Outside, life burgeoned, fresh and strong and straight, whilst in the fetid air of our compartment lurked a blight that sickened and twisted everything it touched. Already I was exhausted again. The simple act of constantly moving from my world to Holmes's and back again, as I had to every moment, was in itself debilitating to an extent I had not foreseen. Thank God I had the cocaine to help me! But its spell was wearing off, and I needed privacy to renew the dose. I lit a cigar and chewed anxiously on the smoke. How dangerously demoralising it was to turn from those stilly gathered oast-houses to confront a man capable of brutally murdering a young mother, bottling her gravid womb, and then celebrating this infamy with a diabolical pastiche of one of our finest Christmas hymns!

We roared through Chatham and Sittingbourne, and still Holmes spoke not a word. As we passed Faversham he roused himself at last, crossed to the outside of the compartment and tried the door. It was locked. He took out his keychain, and opened a small instrument which was attached to it. With this he worked at the lock for a few minutes. Then he reached up and pulled the alarm cord.

'Climb out on the running-board, Watson. When I shout, we jump.'

He opened the door. The brakes were squealing viciously but the train was still moving very fast.

'After you, Holmes.'

With a shrug, he went. Gingerly I followed him out on to the narrow board, clinging for support to the brass handholds. The train was now slowing perceptibly, although the cinder bed beneath us was still but a streak. It was very awkward having to hold my bag while grasping the shaking carriage, and I was wondering how long I would be able to keep it up when Holmes shouted and was gone. I shut my eyes and leapt out into space. The fall was painful, but I was soon on my feet and running towards Holmes, who stood beckoning to me from the abutment of a bridge some fifty yards away. In the other direction the train was grinding to a halt as I joined my companion. Together we climbed the bank, slipped through a hedge, and started off along a little country lane. A short walk brought us to the village of Chartham, where we repaired to the inn. After a leisurely lunch we remade our plans in consultation with Bradshaw. By leaving Holmes for a few minutes at table I was able to restore my flagging energy and confidence, and the day ended without further ado in our sailing aboard the night packet from Newhaven.

I do not propose to weary my readers with a detailed account of our peregrinations through France and Germany. The journey from London to the coast was the model upon which all our subsequent travel was undertaken, and if I had the strength and the time I might compile a catalogue of moonlight flits, assumed identities, invisible foes, arrangements continually revised, and many and various laws infringed. But such a task would be tiresome and nothing to the point. All that matters is that at no time during these five days was Holmes out of my sight, and at no time was I able to bring about the decisive confrontation that I sought. The affair was clearly going to be more difficult than I had imagined. The new month saw us quitting Geneva for the Valais, and found me facing a problem which might aptly be described as insoluble—how to replace my dwindling supply of cocaine. I had only to go to a chemist's and purchase a quantity of the hydrochloride, which I could then dilute at will. But as I have said, at no time during the five days was Sherlock Holmes out of my sight, as a consequence of which I was at no time out of his. I devised several stratagems to obtain the drug secretly, but they all failed. Meanwhile I was having to inject ever larger doses of the solution to maintain that state of vigilance which was so essential, for as I continued to deny my body its rightful rest, so it increased the interest it exacted on the mounting debt.

Had some Olympian observer been following our progress, he must have been mightily amused at the contrast between my expectations that morning in Baker Street and the reality which was unfolding. I had imagined myself—strong, righteous and resolved—leading the bewildered and distraught Holmes to a deserted spot where, man to man, we would have things out. Instead, a Holmes who arose each morning still fitter and more lucid than he had been the day before was dragging his increasingly weakened and distracted companion across Europe on an itinerary which he refused to discuss towards a destination he declined to disclose. In short, with each day that passed we resembled more and more the Holmes and Watson of old. The crisis came when our departure from Geneva—at three o'clock in the morning, in a cart full of empty milk churns—ruled out the last possibility of my obtaining further supplies of cocaine. I had just three days' stock remaining. A few hours after failing to refresh my blood with the drug I would undergo a nervous collapse, and for the next two or three days I would be quite incapable of looking after myself, never mind Holmes. Thus I now knew that the *dénouement* could on no account be delayed beyond the fourth day of May.

On Saturday the 2nd we walked from Leuk to Kandersteg over the Gemmi Pass. I am told the route is extremely scenic. The condition of my nerves, to say nothing of my ankle, prevented me from forming an opinion on the subject. Holmes quite made up for my low spirits, however, displaying a vitality and an exuberance that were almost excessive. We were accompanied by a guide the entire distance, and any initiative on my part was therefore impossible. I remember Holmes making much of a rock-fall which occurred quite close to our path. He clearly regarded the incident as another attempt on his life, and would have none of the guide's protestations that such mishaps were common at that season. After spending the night at Kandersteg, we descended the next morning to Spiez, where Holmes announced that we might indulge in the luxury of public transport for the rest of the day. We accordingly took the steamer to Brienz, continuing that evening by train to Meiringen, where we put up at the Englischer Hof.

As I kept my vigil through the long alpine night, I knew that the morrow must inevitably witness either the success or the failure of my enterprise. Fortunately for me the proprietor of the inn, one Peter Steiler, had worked for some time at the Grosvenor Hotel, and his command of English was excellent. Early the next morning, while Holmes was still asleep, I found Steiler greeting the dawn from the porch of the hotel with a series of yodelling yawns. I engaged him in conversation concerning the noteworthy sights in the locality, and as a result I was able to suggest to Holmes over breakfast that we walk across the hills to Rosenlaui that day, taking in the famous Reichenbach falls on our way. Holmes replied, as was his wont, that such had in fact been his intention. I excused myself, and in the privacy of our room I drew the last dregs of cocaine solution from its bottle and injected it into my scarred forearm. Once again I savoured the gush of strength and clarity and purpose. All was well. The die was cast. Vengeance was to be mine.

To my chagrin and dismay, however, Holmes absolutely refused to start our expedition until after lunch. We had been ceaselessly on the move for nine days, he pointed out, and a morning's rest would do us both good. The walk to Rosenlaui was a matter of a few hours only. We would enjoy a pleasant lunch at the Englischer Hof and set out about two o'clock. I was furious. This whim of Holmes's posed a serious threat to the success of my efforts, since it prevented me forcing a conclusion while the stimulating effects of the drug were at their height. I argued, I cajoled, I begged, I sulked, but all in vain. The pictures I painted of charming picnics in alpine meadows, a bottle of Neuchâtel cooling in a near-by stream, entirely failed to move Holmes. He had made up his mind to spend the morning in Meiringen and that was that. And so I was obliged to fritter away my precious energy on such all-important activities as admiring our landlord's collection of wood-carvings, and listening to Holmes hold forth upon the effect of climate in forming the character of nations.

It was after two o'clock when we finally set out. I was silent, husbanding my strength for the trial that lay ahead. My companion, by contrast, was at his blithest and wittiest. Undeterred by my preoccupation, he persevered gamely in pointing out to me the many beauties of the surrounding landscape. But I was conscious only of the sickening sagging of my spirits, and of the exhaustion and delirium lurking like a pack of wolves at the fringes of my mind.

We had covered about half the distance to the falls when I discovered, with much annoyance, that I had left my watch at the inn. Quite apart from its actual value, the piece was of some considerable sentimental interest to me, having belonged to my late father. I could not feel easy, I told Holmes, until I had it once more in my pocket. But it is always tedious to retrace one's footsteps, and there was no point in his returning with me to Meiringen. I therefore suggested that he continue alone to the falls, where I would rejoin him as soon as possible. Holmes readily agreed, and we parted. I hurried off down the hillside, hoping that I had not made a mistake in letting Holmes out of my sight. But I did not see how else the affair could be managed. I reached Meiringen in a little under the half-hour. Steiler was lounging on the porch of the inn as I hurried up.

'I trust she is no worse?' I cried.

The good old Swiss gazed at me with an expression of stolid puzzlement.

'Worse?'

'The sick Englishwoman! Come, man, lead me to her!'

Steiler's puzzlement darkened to utter confusion.

'There is no Englishwoman staying here!' he exclaimed. 'What are you talking about?'

For answer, I thrust a letter under his nose. It was written upon the stationery of the Englischer Hof and explained that shortly after Holmes and I had left for the falls, an English lady had arrived in the last stages of consumption. Nothing could ease her final hours so much as the presence of an English doctor, and if I would have the goodness to return, etc., etc. The letter was signed 'Peter Steiler'. That individual was now evidently reading it for the first time.

'A Swiss lad came running after us with this letter,' I explained. 'Of course, I could hardly refuse such a request. But now you tell me—'

The situation proved too much for the honest Switzer's carefully cultivated English.

'This is not my write!' he burst out. 'This is not my signing! My paper, yes, but that makes nothing. You should look to—'

But I did not stay for the landlord's suggestions. I had pressing business elsewhere, and besides, the author of the letter was well known to me. I hurried back up the path leading to the Reichenbach falls. My watch, which had apparently been safely tucked away in my fob all the while, showed that it was now twenty past three. Almost eight hours had elapsed since I prematurely injected the last of the cocaine, and it was a miracle that I was still on my feet. No doubt it was the air that was the saving of me. Under England's clouded skies I must have succumbed, but that alpine atmosphere, so piercingly pure and cool, seemed to revive my flagging spirits with every breath. The landscape, too, helped me to concentrate. At those rarefied heights one might as well be on the moon for any sense one has of the operative pressures of civilisation. My mind, weakened by its long dependence on the drug, was already subject to mild hallucinations, but in an odd way these too served my purpose. At times I seemed to be climbing through the painted lumber of a theatre set, like some abstraction from an old morality; no longer 'Good old Watson', but Revenge with his dagger.

Such notions no doubt seem fanciful, set down in cold print. I can only say that they sustained me through that long dizzying climb from Meiringen to the falls at Reichenbach. When I reached my destination, at long last, my only anxiety was that Holmes might have given me the slip. Nor was I immediately reassured, for at first glance there was no sign of him. Then I observed the path which has been cut into the rock half-way around the falls, to afford a better prospect of that attraction. Even a man of steady nerves might well have thought twice before venturing out on to that narrow ledge. In my condition, with my head yawing and spinning, it was harrowing in the extreme. But all my trials seemed worthwhile when, coming in view of the falls, I beheld Sherlock Holmes standing there with his back to the rock and his arms folded, gazing down at the rushing waters. A yard beyond, the path ended abruptly. With grim satisfaction I realised that I now commanded the only exit from the trap in which Holmes had so obligingly placed himself.

I inched towards him, hugging the cliff-wall. The rock was wet and treacherous from the spray hurled up by the water plunging to destruction in the abyss below.

The noise was terrific. I had approached within six feet of Holmes before some intuition of my presence caused him to look up. As soon as his eyes met mine I felt all my mastery ebbing away. I had counted on everything but that terrible look. How utterly mistaken I had been in thinking it would be possible to discountenance Sherlock Holmes! One might sooner have hoped to surprise the Sphinx. The next moment my ankle had given way, causing me to lurch towards the brink of the precipice. I recovered my balance just as Holmes started towards me, his hand outstretched in aid. At once I produced my revolver, and flourished it in his face.

'Back! Back, I say! Another step and I shoot! I mean it, Holmes! Keep your distance. If you come at me, I will not hesitate to fire! This is fair warning. I am in deadly earnest. Stay exactly where you are!'

'Very well, Doctor. I think you have made your point.'

We both had to shout in order to be heard above the howling of the liquid inferno. Holmes stood still, a mocking smile playing on his lips. He made to reach into his coat.

'If we are just going to stand here, you can have no objection if I take a pinch of snuff?'

'Leave it be! Leave it alone!'

I was barely able to hold the gun up. The rock at my feet seemed to be attracting the metal with some magnetic force against which I had constantly to struggle. My reason was hopelessly confused, and my senses prey to delusions of ever-increasing potency. I seemed to hear human voices calling to me from the abyss. With an effort I pulled myself together.

'It's all over, Holmes! I've been in the empty house. I know everything.'

My voice had faded to a whisper. Holmes cupped his ear.

'I beg your pardon?'

'I said, I know everything!'

He smiled indulgently.

'Come my dear fellow, no one knows everything! Not even me.'

The two sides of the waterfall had now parted company. They were swaying in different directions, as if the rock walls were two bones and the water a strip of gristle holding them together. Banshee voices were calling to me from out of the abyss, trying to pass on some vital message which I could not understand since they were speaking it backwards.

'It's no use, Holmes, I've found the evidence. The jars! The papers! I know you killed them.'

'Which? The jars? Or the papers? Or both, perhaps?'

As I gazed up at that urbane and untroubled countenance, I felt my last grip on reality loosening. Could it possibly be true? Could the man standing before me conceivably be Jack the Ripper? What hideous mistake had I made? Where had I gone wrong? Was Moriarty even now watching from the other side of the falls, laughing sardonically? At once, sardonic laughter filled the air. It seemed, though, to be coming from Holmes. But then, of course, Holmes *was* Moriarty!

'Might I trouble you to speak up, Doctor? I can hardly hear you. It would be a pity if your apothegms were to go for nothing.'

A wave of delirium swept through me. In a few moments it would overpower me completely. I raised my voice in desperation.

'Would you still deny it? What's the point? I tell you I know. I know! I know! I know! I watched you butcher Mary Kelly and I've read your unspeakable verses on the subject. The game is up! Try to understand! You are a homicidal maniac! A deranged killer!'

To my horror, Holmes's response to this was one of amusement. His laughter was long and unforced.

'Ah! Do forgive me,' he cried at last. 'It is really too funny for words! Put yourself in my shoes for a moment. Ever since we left London, my companion has been injecting himself thrice daily with ever larger quantities of cocaine. Today he invents a transparently specious excuse to return alone to Meiringen, thus establishing an alibi. On his return he corners me on a dangerous path, produces a pistol, and threatens to shoot me down. Finally—wild-eyed, hysterical, muttering to himself, and generally exhibiting all the symptoms of a drug addict deprived of his dose—he staggers before me, brandishing his weapon, and accuses me of being a deranged killer. Now is my disordered reason misleading me or is there something fundamentally incongruous in this scene?'

'Shut up, Holmes! Shut up! Just shut up! Words, words, words! You can't talk your way out of this. I know what I know. So do you, don't you?'

Holmes shook his head pityingly.

'Say it Holmes! Let me hear it from your own lips!'

'What is it you want me to say?'

'Say you killed them!'

'You killed them.'

'In thirty seconds from now I am going to shoot you! You are about to die. Make your confession, man, and go with some show of remorse, at least. Have you none? Those poor helpless women! Do you want to spend eternity listening to them wail and whine at you from out of the pit? And what about me? Am I never to know the truth? Have a little mercy, Holmes, for Christ's sake!'

He crossed his arms on his chest.

'You're mad, Doctor, and your drivel disgusts me. Pull the trigger and be damned to you!'

I think I was able to do it finally because he had commanded me. I fired. The shot missed him. I steadied myself, but somehow the second bullet also went astray. I fired again. This time I was sure the gun was on target, but the projectile did not strike him. I wondered if the barrel was blocked. I took a step towards that maddeningly invulnerable figure, and fired twice more. Without effect! I felt the hairs on my scalp rising. What manner of witchery was this? From the appalling gulf rose a clammy vapour, and with it the shrieks of the damned. In that arena, sealed off by walls of sound, I stood impotent and alone with a mocking murderer. With a cry of sheer desperation I hurled myself forward, pressed the muzzle of my pistol into his body, and jerked the trigger again and again. The gun fired one last time and fell silent. I plunged headlong into a wall of black exhaustion.

'Snuff?'

I was lying on my side in a puddle of mud. Holmes stood before me, holding out the horn snuffbox. I stared blankly up at him. He inhaled deeply, and gave a grunt of satisfaction.

'Well, now you have had your say we can get down to business. Tell me, when did you kill Watson?'

I continued to stare vacantly at Holmes. For a while he began to sprout a multitude of limbs, like an Oriental deity, but that did not last. Hours later, it seemed, a question formed in my shattered brain.

'Why aren't you dead?'

'Ah, you find that puzzling, do you? Let's see if we can throw some light on it. As two of the finest minds in Europe I shall be surprised if we cannot manage something between us. *Prima facie* there seem to be but three possible explanations: you missed; I am superhuman; there were no bullets. The first, I think you will agree, can be dismissed at once. Even the worst shot in the world, with a head as addled as yours, could hardly have failed with that last attempt. The second—alas!— must also be rejected. It follows then, does it not, that someone must have replaced the live cartridges in your revolver with blanks. I would not be above suspecting myself, quite honestly. All right? Good. Then let us return to the matter in hand. I repeat, when did you kill Dr Watson?'

There were now clearly two Holmeses. One stood talking to me on the path, while the other hovered a few feet away in the spray above the falls, and said nothing.

'Look Moriarty, this will have to stop, you know. No one could be a greater admirer of your skills than myself, but this really isn't the time or place. Your impersonation of my friend is quite first-rate, agreed. The boards of the West End are yours for the asking, always assuming you manage to leave here alive. Nevertheless, good as you were, you weren't quite good enough! Mind you, the task was formidable. I knew my Watson very well indeed, and your performance—though enormously talented—just failed to convince, in the final analysis. Your externals could hardly be bettered, and you even managed to limp with the correct leg this time, but where was the spirit? Sadly lacking! Where was the air of dog-like devotion so characteristic of my dear friend? Where was his obedient good-nature, his ready sympathy, his generous emotion, his well-meant if blundering initiatives? In whatever may be measured and calculated, Professor, you excelled, like the great mathematician you are. But you are no artist, and the soul of the man eluded you utterly. However, you disguised your features, you could not disguise that sense of your own destiny, that knowledge of your power which informs everything you do. The difficulties you faced were perhaps greater than ever you had realised. How much easier it is for a dullard to ape the trappings of genius than for a brilliant man successfully to put on mediocrity!'

The infernal choir was now echoing every word Holmes spoke. In vain I shook my head and beat my temples. The inexorable voice ground on.

'To be fair, though, my suspicions were aroused right from the beginning, when I found you stealthily returning my keychain that morning in Kensington. Why would Watson need my keys? And if he had, would he not take them openly? From that moment I was on my guard. When I asked the maid to fetch a cab she mentioned a letter you had just given her to post. I relieved her of it, and was amused to find a note to the police, accusing me of the Whitechapel murders! I don't imagine your absurd charges and trumped-up evidence would get much of a hearing at Scotland Yard, but to save myself needless bother I simply brought the thing away with me.'

He produced a long slim envelope from his pocket. With a cry of utter despair I recognised the extent of my failure.

'Too bad, isn't it?' agreed Holmes. 'But how like you, Moriarty, to hedge your bets! Even if I got the better of you in person, you were counting on posthumous revenge!'

With a careless gesture he flicked the envelope out into the void.

'Shortly thereafter,' he continued, 'I discovered your bottle of cocaine, and finally—it was in Brussels—I was able to observe you actually injecting the drug into your arm. From that moment, of course, I had no further doubts. If any two things in this life may be taken as absolutely certain, they are that Dr Watson is as incapable of adopting such a habit as Professor Moriarty is of abandoning it. By the same token, you were from that moment completely in my power. I had only to prevent you from obtaining more of the drug, which you could not buy openly without revealing your true identity, and eventually, as happened this morning, the exigencies of your addiction would force your hand. Knowing when the blow would fall, I could take my precautions to parry it effectively. Incidentally, it may interest you to know that the snuff in this box derives its virtues from *Erythroxylon cocoa* rather than *Nicotiana tabacum*. A pinch a day, as the saying goes, keeps the doctor at bay. How many hours is it now since you took your medicine, Moriarty? I hope you don't mind me saying that you look a trifle peaky.'

The blood in my veins, it seemed, had turned to lice,* whose pulsating passage through my body was making my skin crawl. The voice, meanwhile, continued to come at me from all sides.

'The only point on which I am still uncertain is just when you did away with my faithful Watson. I assume it was during that night when in a moment of criminal weakness I allowed myself to indulge my exhaustion,

*Sic.

and when he—poor innocent man—put me to bed instead of ruthlessly turning me out of doors, as he should. Was that the occasion, Moriarty? You would have had no difficulty in getting into the house, and Watson would have been clay in your hands! You might have killed me too, as I slept, but that would not have satisfied your devious and diseased genius. Instead, having murdered my friend, you had the brilliant notion of taking his place. How you must have laughed at my attempts to shake off a man who all the while was seated at my side! Yes indeed, that must have diverted you no end. But once I was sure of you, I too had my fun! It has been a pleasure, I assure you, dragging you out of bed in the small hours, pulling you through windows and pushing you off trains! How maddening for you it must have been, knowing it was all a farce. And then your growing realisation that our route was exactly the same as in 1888, when it was I who followed you. But you could hardly mention that, either! How very frustrating! And now this *bouleversement* on top of everything else! I fear it has not been your week, Professor. But have you nothing to say, now you can speak freely? Still this unwonted silence? As you will! You shall shortly be silent indeed. As silent as the grave. Oh yes, no fear of your returning from the dead this time! For this occasion, if you permit it, I intend to take a tip from the master himself.'

From the depths of his coat, Holmes produced a thin packet wrapped in oil-cloth. He undid the string and unrolled the cloth. A gasp of sheer mortal terror escaped me as he lifted from its bindings a six-inch post-mortem knife.

'Recognise it, do you? I took the liberty of visiting your little hideaway in Baker Street before I called on Watson. I brought this away with me, concealed in the lining of my coat. Since we are to have justice at last, it might as well be poetic.'

'But Holmes! You—'

His voice cut across my stutterings like a whiplash.

'*Mister* Holmes, if you please. Let us preserve the proprieties.'

'But this is me, Holmes! Watson! I am Watson!'

'You just don't give up, do you? Admirable trait under normal circumstances of course, but in questionable taste for one who is but seconds away from meeting his Maker.'

Raising his dreadful weapon, he stepped towards me. There was no question of me defending myself. Even under normal conditions Holmes was more than a match for me. In my present state there could be no contest. In a few moments I would be lying at the bottom of the falls with my throat cut, and Jack the Ripper would be free to resume his interrupted career.

'Holmes, I am Watson! I am your friend Watson! I have only tried to save you from yourself, and from the indignities of the law. My only thought has been to save you!'

Holmes's boot sent me sprawling on my back. He knelt at my side, holding me down with one hand. The other raised the knife to strike. I screamed my last words above the din of the falls.

'He has fooled you, Holmes! You have become Moriarty's creature! He made you think that I am he, and now you are doing his work for him! What a victory! To trick the great Sherlock Holmes into murdering his only true and loving friend! What a triumph! He has won! Kill me then, for Moriarty has won! He has won!'

I shut my eyes, awaiting the sudden pain, the darkness and despair.

It did not come. When I opened my eyes again Holmes was still kneeling at my side, but the knife was lowered. He was gazing at me, and his face was filled with an infinite sadness. It was as if he had been granted a vision of universal truth, and had found it sad beyond all telling. I cannot say how long we remained there, nor what wordless communications passed between us. At last Holmes sighed gravely, and got to his feet. He looked down at the knife in his hand. Expressionlessly, he let it fall into the depths behind him. Then he looked down at me once more.

'Never fear, old fellow,' he murmured. 'You shall not be hurt. I shall not let him hurt you.'

With these words he stepped backwards off the edge of the precipice. I crawled to the brink of that fearful abyss and looked over in time to see Holmes's body strike an outcrop of rock far below. Then I knew no more.

## Conclusion

I awoke two days later in a bed at the Englischer Hof, whither I had been conveyed by a party from Meiringen. My unconscious body had been discovered lying at the very edge of the path by the falls, so that the slightest movement must instantly have precipitated me into the yawning depths. On Thursday morning I was interviewed by the Swiss police. They accepted readily enough that my prostration had been caused by the shock of my companion's death, but proved considerably more sceptical when it came to swallowing my story of vanishing youths and criminal masterminds. At length I hit upon the idea of asking Lestrade to confirm my *bona fides,* and following the receipt of a telegram from Scotland Yard the attitude of the local officials changed from guarded suspicion to respectful condolence.

On my return to London a week later I removed the papers and the jars from the empty house in Baker Street. The jars I took to Bart's and there disposed of their hideous contents. The papers I burned. Once these measures had been taken I felt reasonably sure that no one would ever have cause to suspect the truth about Sherlock Holmes's last years. But I wanted to do more than that for my old friend: I wanted to perpetuate the good that was in him before the darkness overshadowed it. Above all I wanted to impress upon the public mind an image of Holmes's honourable life and noble death; an image so attractive and indelible that if any later searcher should stumble on the truth (for I could not be sure that other damning evidence did not exist elsewhere) his accusations would be received with frowns and frigid silence, as being at once tasteless and absurd.

As luck would have it, the perfect sculptor for my monument was at hand. In order to avoid interrupting the course of my narrative, I omitted to mention that A.C.D. had approached me early in 1891 with a view to obtaining further material from my records for Holmes's cases. It seemed that his second foray into this genre had proved sufficiently successful to induce him to continue the experiment, but with a difference. What he now proposed was to write a series of short tales, each devoted to one of Holmes's successes. As I have said, I was out of touch with Holmes at this time, but in view of his ready agreement on the previous occasion I had no hesitation in selecting twelve cases which I felt illustrated various aspects of my friend's genius and passing these on to A.C.D. In the fury of the events which followed closely thereafter I forgot all about this new literary venture.

A.C.D.'s stories started to appear in the *Strand*'s July issue. They were immediately successful, and with every month that passed the demand for the magazine increased. A.C.D.'s response to this triumph was typically ambivalent. On the one hand he could not help being pleased that his work was so popular; on the other he feared that the very success of the stories was keeping him from more serious and worthy endeavours. The news of Sherlock Holmes's death showed him a way out of this dilemma. Early in 1892 he came to see me and proposed that I furnish him with the material for a further twelve tales, the last of which was to be an account of the events leading up to Holmes's death at the Reichenbach falls. This would effectively terminate the series and free A.C.D. from the temptation of indulging further in work he had come to regard as menial if lucrative drudgery.

The suggestion could not have fitted in better with my own desires, and I set to work with a will. Eleven of the dozen cases were no trouble to prepare, since I had only to collate and copy out in a fair hand my already-existing notes. But when it came to dealing with Holmes's death I was faced with the singular problem of inventing a plausible series of events which would satisfy the known facts, yet reveal nothing of the terrible truth behind them. I fear I did not manage to concoct a very convincing smoke-screen. Indeed, a close reading of the finished story—which A.C.D. entitled, more aptly than he knew, 'The Final Problem'—will reveal that it is riddled with inconsistencies. But it is part of the business of a good writer to prevent his audience from reading closely if this does not suit his purposes, and when the tale finally appeared any question of its weaknesses went unheard in the general howl of dismay that Holmes was dead and the series at an end. Never had there been such an outcry! A.C.D.'s readers had come to think of Holmes as a valued and trusted friend. My wishes could not have been more fully realised.

Later, of course, A.C.D. saw fit to start writing detective stories again, and since the public has no use for dead heroes he was obliged to bring Holmes back to life in another apocryphal adventure, which I may say I think has the distinction of being even less probable than the one I devised. But by then Holmes had ceased to be remembered as a real figure, except by a small circle of acquaintances. He had become a fictional character. I have no complaint to make at this turn of

events. It was after all Holmes himself who, by his infamies, effectively removed himself from the ranks of
mankind. Thereafter he was doomed to become either a
myth or a monster. Fortunately I was able to ensure
that it was the former. Perhaps, indeed, the myth I
helped to create has taken such powerful hold on the
public imagination that the facts, once they can be
safely revealed, will not be credited. So be it! I had
rather be taken for a fraud, than have seen the many for
whom Sherlock Holmes was an ideal and an example
shattered and embittered on learning the horrible truth
about their paragon.

For myself, the cost was not light. I returned from
Switzerland in broken health, and with a craving for
further injections of cocaine which took more than two
years to mend. By then my practice was once more in
ruins, and although I benefited substantially by Holmes's
will, my wife and I were in financial straits for some
time. But others have recently made far greater sacri-
fices for our country, and it would ill become me to
complain of my lot.

And so my narrative is finally at an end. Since
Holmes's death my existence has been a quiet and commonplace one. But sometimes, as I sit by the fire on
nights when the wind wails in the chimney, my thoughts
travel back to the great falls at Reichenbach, and I hear
again the exquisite consolation of Holmes's final words,
and see once more the light of understanding in his
eyes, during those last moments when he seemed once
again the best and the wisest man I have ever known.

'Any attempt at recovering the bodies was absolutely hopeless, and there, deep down in that
dreadful cauldron of swirling water and seething
foam, will lie for all time the most dangerous criminal and the foremost champion of the law of their
generation.'

SIR ARTHUR CONAN DOYLE:
*The Final Problem*

# Afterword

❧

'To the concept of the Son, which seemed exhausted, he
added the complexities of evil and misfortune,' writes
Borges of Nils Runeberg, the Swedish theologian who
argued that the Saviour was not Jesus Christ but Judas
Iscariot ('Three Versions of Judas' in *Labyrinths,* Pen-
guin, 1970). Some disciples of the Master will no doubt
accuse me of an equivalent heresy. But it should at least
be obvious that, like Runeberg's, mine is the blasphemy
of the true believer.

Anyone wishing to compose variations on the Canon
must first decide which authority to follow on questions
of chronology. My guide throughout has been D. Mar-
tin Dakin, whose conclusions are supported with
weighty and lucid arguments in his book *A Sherlock
Holmes Commentary* (David & Charles, 1972). My
epigraph is taken from James Edward Holroyd's introduction to *Seventeen Steps to 221B* (Allen & Unwin,
1967), which is edited by him and contains various entertaining and informative essays. It would be impossible to exaggerate my indebtedness to *The Annotated
Sherlock Holmes* (John Murray, 1968), edited by William Baring-Gould, whose two volumes constitute a
splendid lucky-dip *de luxe* for anyone whose interest in
the stories extends beyond the simple desire to know
who done it.

I consulted various sources for information on the Whitechapel murders, but found little of consequence that is not included in *The Complete Jack the Ripper* (W. H. Allen, 1975.). Donald Rumbelow surveys all the existing evidence and theories with an impartiality virtually unique in a field dominated by writers who have discovered The Answer.

I should not like to close without mentioning the late J. L. Stonier, but for whom this book would not have been written. He was himself an admirer of the Holmes stories, and I like to think he might have granted that the pastiche he helped to make possible was 'not entirely devoid of certain features of interest'.

M.J.D.

*Chiswick*
*December 1977*

## ABOUT THE AUTHOR

Born in 1947, Michael Dibdin attended schools in
Scotland and Ireland, and universities in England
and Canada. He taught for a short while at Vancouver
Free University, and now lives in London with his
wife and daughter.